chained

blackstone gates series

K.L. STEELE

Copyright Chained© 2024 by K.L. Steele

All rights reserved.

No portion of this book may be reproduced in any form or by any electronic or mechanical means, including information storage and retrieval systems without written permission from the author except for the use of brief quotations for the purpose of a book review.

This is a work of fiction. Names, characters, places, and incidents either are the product of the author's imagination or are used fictitiously. Any resemblance to actual persons, living or dead, events, or locales is entirely coincidental.

First Edition Edited by: Villain Era Book Services

Second Edition Edited by: Alexa at The Fiction Fix

Cover design by: © Dez Purington @ Pretty in Ink Creations

Artwork by: Priska (@Priska_art)

This one is for the readers who know what they want and how they want it.

CONTENT WARNING

Before you venture further into the world of Blackstone Gates, there are a few things to note. This book is a few shades darker than the first in the series, so please take some time to check over the content warnings below. Chained is intended for audiences above the age of 18 years. Your mental health is incredibly important.

This book contains, but is not limited to:

Explicit sex scenes
- Kidnapping
- Attempted SA- Not by the MCs
- Parental neglect/emotional abuse
- Blood play
- Light gore
- Graphic Violence
- Hand necklaces/breath play
- Chase scenes
- Sharp object play

Pain play
Acts in monster form
Multiple partners
Reference to twincest- Not MCs
Satan/demons

CHAPTER 1
PYRO

Silence.

Or it would be, if I couldn't hear the grinding teeth and heaving breaths from the twins beside me. All three of us are rooted to the spot, staring at the space Wynn stood just moments ago. The space is now filled with dark green smoke and a smell that's uniquely hers. Sweet ambrette fills my flared nostrils, and I take in as much of her scent as I can. Fuck knows when we will be able to get close to her again. We need to get to her, but we need to be smart about it. The twins are not known for the ability to control their impulses, and to be honest, neither am I.

Of all demons, Lev isn't the one you want to fuck with. He has influence in Hell, with a horde of hellhounds willing to do his bidding. His methods are archaic in nature, with his best interests put before anyone else. He is a true demon created in the name of Envy, a title he wears in a way no one else can.

When a soul is harvested or sent to Hell, it's sorted. Some of the most terrible souls are used for fun—torture, slavery. You name it and there are sure to be demons willing to use them for it. These are the bottom feeders. Once their use is up, they're sent to the depths, never to be seen or heard from again. They're thrown into the deep, swirling pool at the core of Hell, becoming one with the blistering lava.

One step up from this is my kind. Hellhounds. The mercenaries of Hell, still demons but lower in the pecking order. Our souls are handpicked by Grimm, sentenced to a life of guarding the gates and doing the bidding of those who sit above us. Muscle for hire, so to speak. A commodity to be bought and traded if they don't possess the strength to make it on their own.

Lev has the most use for hellhounds as the main gatekeeper of Hell. He's the one who keeps watch of who comes and goes, ensuring the Earth's living plane doesn't get overrun with menace and mayhem. Some hellhounds, like me, prefer to sell our services, moving from place to place with no true home. Taking jobs for any of the seven that we see fit. Others, however, feed off Lev's energy and feel a small sense of loyalty to the demon that 'helps' them through their first few shifts. If you can call any support he provides help.

Tension in the air hangs heavy, each of us waiting for someone to say something. To move. Anything. It takes all the willpower I possess not to tear through the gates of Hell with fire burning through my veins, disintegrating any being that tries to stand in my way.

A few moments is all it took for her to sink those black-painted talons deep into my soul without even trying, completely oblivious to the effect she has not only on me, but these two assholes as well. The physical pull that rips through my body when she's close coaxes my hellhound form to the surface, willing it to toy with the darkness inside her. Hundreds of years, I have practiced my control, and all it takes is one glance from her to tear it to shreds with a devilish grin.

The strong, metallic scent of blood floods the room,

slowly dripping on the floor beside me. Searching for the source, I find Bale's black lengthened claws pulsing into his now jagged palms in perfect unison with the grind of his teeth. Small pieces of flesh flay from the rough slices, gnarly and raw. One of our similarities, it seems—the use of pain to regain control.

He's the first to move, storming into the room and grasping the closest piece of furniture he can reach. Wood splinters fly across the room, a tornado made of flesh and bone, ripping into everything in his path until he reaches the source of her scent. A dark blanket of fur pools on the ground beside the bed, the same one he placed along her back to keep her warm earlier in the night. Picking it up, he brings it to his face and breathes in the remnants of her scent, his blood melding with the lingering scent of our little mate.

"I'm going to fucking kill him!" he roars, his bright amber eyes focused on the blanket in his hands. Pure rage rolls off his shaking body, shakes that are slowly starting to subside with each inhale. Without even being here, she calms him. It took mere days for each of us to become obsessed with our human, the fates gifting us and fucking us over in one hit.

The faster we get to Hell and into the ring of Wrath with Satan, the twins' father, the faster we will get back to her. Getting that through to Bale without incident is going to be nearly impossible, though. One wrong move will be all it takes for Lev to kill her, regardless of her worth.

Bale and his father have never gotten along, that's no secret. Anyone who ever saw the pair came to expect a show, and Hell isn't a place to stop the mayhem of two alpha males fighting to near death, especially not when it is Satan himself and his vampire son.

Luka walks further into the room, stepping over the carnage like it is nothing. This side of Bale must be something he is used to because he doesn't bat an eye. He simply sits on one of the arm chairs with his large, bat-like wings stretching out either side while he settles into place. "How the fuck do we get our little mate back?"

"We go down there and take her. Should be able to get an in somehow if Axton stays the fuck out of our way," Bale growls, stalking back toward me, kicking the timber in his path until we stand face to face. "And you. *You* are going to help us fix the mess you created."

He's angry and frustrated, looking for someone to blame. I get it, but that someone isn't me. I try to tamper down the anger flowing through my fingertips, a shift once again threatening to break through. My jaw burns, fire slowly igniting my bones. The last thing we need is to be fighting each other.

"What do you mean, *I created*?" I breathe through clenched teeth, attempting to control my tone. Little shit has no self-preservation skills; one fucking swipe, and I could gut him. I won't, because that would cause Wynn pain now that they are bonded, but he's pushing it.

He moves closer, his cool breath fanning across my face with his snarl. "If it wasn't for you making us leave the room, he wouldn't have been able to get to her in the first place, asshole. So yes. *You*."

My hand moves quickly, grasping his corded throat and slamming him into the edge of the doorway with enough force to break the wood. He thrashes in my hold, kicking his boots at me, claws raking across my forearms. Blood and smoke seeps from the wounds marring my skin, creating a thick haze between us.

Through his temper tantrum, my body stays completely still, giving not even a twitch. I take every bit of his brutality, momentarily enjoying the feeling flowing through my veins. Bale may have been born into royalty, but I am a hell of a lot older than him. If this is going to work, he is going to need to learn a thing or two about dynamics. Lesson number one: don't be a dick to beings are on the same fucking side.

"Stop. *Now*!" I snap, lifting him higher by the throat. My nostrils flare at the familiar scent of burnt skin, the heat of my palm searing through layers of skin and flesh with ease. A delicate dance between fire and ice, a creature created in the eyes of Hell and the spawn of the damned. His pulse races beneath my firmly planted thumb, thrumming out of control as his life hangs in the balance.

"You made us leave the room, and she was taken, Pyro," Bale chokes back, the black veins under his eyes spreading rapidly beneath his near-translucent skin. He's going to need an outlet, one that I will gladly help with once we're a step closer to getting our mate back. His father is the Prince of Wrath, with access to fighting pits and lackey demons at any time of day. If it is a fight he needs, I will give him one, but not here and not now, however tempting it may be.

"Leviathan is much older than the three of us combined and much more powerful. If we were in there with her, we would likely be burning piles of ash, charring the floor. Then we would truly be fucking useless to her. Would you like that, fangs?"

Bale's jaw flexes as his fangs start to retract, raw anger racking through his rigid body as he practically vibrates in my hold, taking every single piece of his will power to not react and tear my skin from my flesh. Emotion this strong could give me a decent high if circumstances were different. But here we are, sober and no closer to getting her back.

"He's right, brother," Luka adds, his eyes glowing a few shades lighter as they fix on where my hand grips his twin. His crimson gaze moves to mine, nodding toward my hands. "It feels real good to try and kill him when he's being an asshole, but I think he secretly likes it."

"If I let you go, will you stop?" I question, loosening my

grip slightly. Bale nods, his eyes flitting between mine and Luka's. "Let's get down there and talk to your dad. We can't go barging into Lev's home demanding shit. We need a plan. Even your emotionally immature ass knows that. Childish at times, but not stupid."

Bale's nostrils flare as he pushes into my hand, forcing me to step back with my hand still wrapped around his throat. It has hurt, the welts warm under my fingers. Surface wounds like this will heal with time, but he gives me nothing, not a single twitch.

"Touch me like this again, and I will make good on my promise from yesterday. I would love nothing more than to tear your spine out through your fucking mouth, dog boy. If messing with the treaty is what needs to happen to get her back, we do it with no hesitation," he snarls, his lip curling in disgust.

"Ahh, there he is, back to the moody asshole we know and love. Thought we lost you for a bit there," Luka calls, rising from the chair and maneuvering his way back through the room to stand to my right. "Come on, let's get home, and you two can fight it out in the pits. You are going to have to learn to play nice if we have any chance of getting our girl back."

My hand drops to my side, taking bits of burnt skin with it. I reach down, dusting the charred remains of Bale's throat onto my black, Kevlar jeans. The corners of my lips tip into a grin at the thought of fighting the angry little shit down there.

I can't wait. All of this pent up tension, ready to explode.

The darkened tunnels below the academy are stale, barely used unless the twins go back home or their father comes up to see them. Demons and monsters do not have access to the tunnels, with blood bonds being the only thing that will open the heavy stone doors. Luckily, the twins have open access.

We have been walking in silence since we left the twins' wing, with Bale back to pulsing his claws in his palms. Only now, he has a small piece of black lace entwined in his fingers. By the scent, I am assuming those are our little mate's panties. Why he is covering them in blood and carrying them around, I have no idea.

Our footsteps are the only sounds down here, echoing through the darkness. Small stones crunch under our heavy boots as we descend further into the tunnel, the ground slowly transitioning to loose gravel the deeper we go. My body thrums with excitement, sensing we are closer to home, the need to shift clawing at my bones from the inside out. Intense hellfire flows through my veins, reaching my skin within seconds. My hellhound side is forcing itself out whether I want to or not it seems.

Stopping dead in my tracks, I wait until they are both a few steps ahead before letting the shift completely take over. It will be easier to cross in my hound form, and hellhounds don't typically walk around here in their human forms anyway. Our more primal state is preferable, with added strength and senses. The meat suits we use are more for the illusion of humanity when required, and for fucking other non-hellhound demons when the need arises. Demons are not human and still can't take the size of us, something that will need to stay reined in around our little mate—though I have a feeling Wynn would be into that sort of shit, and my restraint only goes so far.

Cracking my neck from one side to the other, I stretch myself out to release the tension before the smoke engulfs my body. It forces me down, flash-burning my skin until my hound form completely takes over. Shifting isn't as painful as it seems, not after this many years. Much like getting a tattoo, it burns and feels as though it is slicing through your top layers of skin. It spreads across your entire body for a few seconds, searing you from the inside out, but not enough that you wouldn't go back. It's a rush. Adrenaline on tap.

My heavy paws flex in the gravel, feeling the stones beneath my feet. Little pieces of rock graze my flesh, the small amount of pain helping to calm my thoughts. My thoughts swirl of her, of that sharp tongue of hers pissing off one of the most powerful demons in Hell. I can only imagine the horror on Lev's face when she opens her mouth, spitting venom at a demon who makes his own kind cower. Without someone thinking clearly, we will never get to her in one piece.

Shaking off, I run to catch up to the twins, who look to have both done the same. Luka's wings hang neatly behind him, the ends dragging a trailing line across the stones behind him. Bale looks practically the same as always, just larger. He has been vamping out on and off since she was taken. Fangs obsessively toy with his piercings, cutting his skin and healing it moments later. It makes him look more menacing, blood trailing down each side of his face.

We approach another door with a small, pointed piece of obsidian off to the side and a bowl sitting underneath. Without a word, Bale pricks the end of his finger on the volcanic glass, his blood unlocking the warded entryway. This space is more familiar, unseen to the human eye. Not until they are dead and passing through do they see it, and even then, they are usually too distressed to take any notice. Sensitive little things, those souls, too flighty.

"If these rabid assholes attempt not to let us through, I'm going to gut them one by one," Bale snaps, stepping over the threshold and storming toward the gate. They would have heard him, the hellhounds who guard the gates. If we are lucky, it will be a hellhound I am familiar with on duty, or one who at least knows of me. Then, there may be a chance to talk them down from the explosion Bale is preparing for.

Shaking my head, I step into the cavernous space and take a deep breath. Even from out here, it smells like home. Smoke and stone. Not the kind of smoke that seeps from my pores, but Hell smoke. It is rich and warm, filling my lungs and pulling a low rumble from deep within my chest.

Three hellhounds are already circling Bale, their smoke making his figure slightly hard to make out from a distance, a mass of darkened haze with him at the centre.

"I hear he has her, your pretty little mate," one sneers, ducking his head lower, a shiver running through his body to the tip of his tail. "A real, live human in Hell, what a treat. A treat I would kill for a taste of. I bet she tastes sweet, innocent. The thought is getting me fucking hard. Nice, big hellhound cock to rip her in two."

"Say it again, once more," Bale rasps through clenched fangs, his eyes surrounded by black veins, slowly spinning to follow along with the hellhound who dares speak about her. The hellhound chuckles, shaking his head as he continues to circle. Of course, it had to be Archus. The cocky piece of shit would do anything to climb the ladder and get his nose closer to Lev's asshole. The other two have stepped back, their eyes now focused on Luka and me approaching. I don't recognize them at all, probably some new souls Archus has convinced to follow him. He's not an alpha by any stretch, but he talks a big game for someone so small and insignificant.

"I said, a human in Hell, can't fucking wait to smell her. Wonder if the boss man will let us give her a run-through in hound form. That tight little cunt would struggle to fit my knot, but fuck, it would be nice to try." He grins, his jagged canines almost glowing in the darkness, a stark difference to his jet black fur.

"Archus, fuck off and let us pass. You have no control over

the three of us, none. Crawl back into the hole you came from before vamp boy here lets loose and tears your throat out. He quite likes that," I snarl, stepping in their direction, ready to rip him apart myself if needed. The venom in his words is to taunt us, knowing at least one of the three of us will bite. Bale is an easy target, emotionally strained and pent up with unfiltered rage.

There isn't a doubt in my mind Lev wouldn't let someone like Archus near his new pawn, not until he has done the damage he wants to do with her. Why steal something of worth only to break it so soon? If anything, she will be housed in the Keep, away from the rabid hounds he holds in the lower levels. Worst case, she's in his little forbidden zoo, warded to the nines with impenetrable bars until he wants to display his prize.

No one quite knows the creatures lurking in his prison, other than Silas his right hand hellhound of sorts. Every other being in existence who has seen the inside has ended up in the lower pits, never to be seen again, his secrets taken to their graves.

One look in our direction is all it takes, one single second for chaos to erupt. Luka and I charge toward the two hellhounds off to the side, who start to run toward Bale and their leader. They skid to a stop moments later when faced with the manic beast, the one I knew was there but hadn't seen in the flesh. There in front of us, Bale stands with a beating heart in one hand, Archus' head in the other. A slow smile spreads across his face before he sinks his fangs into the heart and rips it apart, covering the remaining hellhounds in black, tar-like blood. The limp body beneath him turns to smoldering ash, remnants dripping from his fingertips onto the stone floor.

"Anyone else have something to say?" Luka grins, trailing his tail along a hound's back as he circles it to stand beside his brother. The sharpened edge cuts a thin line along its skin, smoke billowing out of the cracks. "Aw. Baby pups. There are plenty more fish in the sea, more decrepit mutts to blindly follow."

One of them snaps his teeth in Luka's direction, growling but otherwise says nothing, his eyes flitting between the twins. The other one steps back half a step, bumping into my shoulder as I walk around them, standing to Bale's other side. We do need an outlet, but as much as tearing them to pieces sounds really fun right now, killing the gatekeepers likely isn't the best option. We need as many on our side as we can get, and so will she if she has any chance of surviving.

"If you want to live to see another day, move the fuck out of our way. Speak one word of her, and your fate will be much worse. Your friend got it quick because Bale had a thirst to quench, but me? I would happily wait and watch the pair of you suffer for weeks on end until you beg me to send you down with the wasted souls, bottom feeders for the rest of your pathetic existence. Do you understand?" I look between them, flames burning behind my eyes.

Without a word, they move away, slipping into the dark corners, leaving the three of us standing before the gates, one step closer to home. A step closer to her.

CHAPTER 2
WYNN

A faint taste of ash lingers on my tongue as I try to breathe, the smoke infiltrating my lungs and forcing a raspy cough from my throat. The roaring sound of fire flows from somewhere beneath me, but the smoke makes it too difficult to see. It's dark, that much I can tell, but otherwise, it is all a haze that stings my eyes each time my eyelids flit open.

My arms tentatively stretch out, feeling the heated stone beneath my body, snapping the ends of a few nails while they drag along the uneven surface. Tears well in the corner of my eyes, threatening to escape at the intense pain flowing through every inch of me. It feels like I have been hit by a truck, one that decided to throw it in reverse and drive over me a second time.

"Welcome to Hell, Wynn. You're going to love it down here," Leviathan laughs from somewhere above me, the glow in his eyes the only thing I can see through the mix of smoke and unshed tears.

If the last twenty-four hours hadn't played out like they did, I would have laughed. But considering just yesterday, my mind was opened to the world of other beings, men with wings and tails, fangs and claws, people who become giant wolves that seep smoke and fire, or who say their name is Satan...

Yet, here I am, stark naked and in pain, laying on the hard ground of what is most likely the Hell he tells me it is. My body is stripped bare, shoved through a mysterious green mist with the threat of death lingering in the air. I've been exposed to lord knows who or what, with no idea about anything around me. I need to block it out and get my wits about me again before even attempting to process what in the world has happened over the last few days.

"If I had any doubts you were human, they are gone watching you struggle with something as simple as breathing. I can't have you dying before the fun has even started," Leviathan taunts, wrapping his searing hand around my throat firmly and pulling me to stand.

"Funny, I thought you wanted me dead," I manage to croak out, my throat dry and scratchy from the thick, smokey air. "Wasn't that the order? Dead or alive, your pet told us, right before the twins killed him."

Each breath I try to suck in puts pressure on my lungs, like forcing mud through a coffee filter. Small amounts get through, but nowhere near enough, heavier and heavier with each inhale. He pushes my body forward as I stumble, my bare feet struggling on the hot, jagged stone. The asshole chuckles behind me, his tone deep and menacing.

"You know, at first, I did. I didn't care whether I got you dead or alive. But I had a moment of clarity, some use for you that went beyond keeping your womb baron. An inkling, shall we say."

"Do you have to be touching me? Where do you think I am going to run to?" I growl, the pain from his heated touch unbearable. I can make out a faint glow in front of us, a misty green hue surrounding what looks to be a tall door. Everything else around me is blurred with smoke and darkness, near impossible to see through.

"You are going to walk through that door into your new life. Well, for the moment anyway," he urges, pushing me toward the door that opens automatically as we get closer.

Tentatively stepping through the entrance, I rub my sore eyes as they adjust to the light. The air is clearer in here, my lungs expanding painfully in an attempt to take a deep breath. My arms move to cover myself, one arm flattened across my chest and the other between my thighs. It won't do much, but it's not like there is any other choice right now. I'm fairly certain he isn't too concerned about my nudity—or my feelings, for that matter—or I wouldn't be down here in the first place.

"This is the Keep, specifically *my* keep," he announces as he steps through the door behind me. "You would do best to stick close. You may hate me but I am safer than the ones who roam these halls. They are loyal, as much as their kind can be, but they are still animals, beasts that would give anything for a taste of human fear, especially when wrapped in a body like yours, begging for sin."

While the darkness has carried through, it is lighter than where we came. Candles sit over stone arches, throwing an orange hue, their flickering flames dancing with the shadows. I can still hear the roar of the fire from below, but it's nowhere near as loud as before. It reminds me of the old movie castles, with the heavy chains bolted into the walls at random intervals, worn wooden beams overhead.

"Not what you were expecting?" he asks, stepping around me, his hand ghosting my lower back, leaving a heated trail. "Of course it wasn't. You know absolutely nothing about our world. A clueless little cum dumpster for the royals to breed. The fates can be cruel, really."

I bite back my response, the inside of my cheeks starting to bleed. He isn't wholly wrong; I know sweet fuck all about this place. I know nothing about the beings here other than what movies, tv shows, and romance books have shown me. Knowing about knotted cocks isn't going to get me out of this situation.

My eyes zone in on the scratch marks in the floor, the gouges deep and erratic, angry. A low snarl rumbles from the darkness ahead, a set of glowing red orbs looking directly at the pair of us.

"Ahh, speaking of the beasts," he laughs, walking ahead of me and toward the noise. Heavy metal chains clink against the stone, echoing through the wide hallway. A shiver works its way through my body from my lower spine to my neck, forcing each little hair to stand on end.

I stumble forward, one foot in front of the other, still a little unsteady on my feet but not wanting to be left behind. He may be the devil incarnate, but he seems to at least want me alive for a short period of time ,which is something I can use to my advantage. A stretch, but something.

"Learn to fucking control yourself, Cassius. You were sent here for a reason. Now, sit down, rein in the hunger, and let the girl pass. If you even attempt to snap, your head will be torn from your body, your soul tossed below to rot with the rest of the scum. I can't have her ruined before they even see her."

Chains once again drag along the ground, the creature in the darkness shifting around before breathing out a loud huff. Leviathan called it Cassius, and whatever Cassius is, it's huge.

"Come, Wynn," Leviathan commands. "Your eyes should have adjusted enough to get you through the hall."

Cassius' red eyes are pinned to me, watching every single movement intently, climbing my entire body and back down again. Every inch of me is exposed, other than the slight coverage my hands provide.

I straighten myself, rolling out my sore shoulders, hearing the crunch of my muscles and bones grinding. No amount of rest will heal this deep seated pain, the burn blooming through my limbs with every movement. I could be wrong, but bath salts and pain relievers don't sound like they would be a staple in the Hell portrayed in popular culture.

A sinister laugh echoes through the space, Leviathan's goading pulling me from my train of thought.

"You have fucked worse monsters than this, girl. Maybe the fates got it wrong after all, and my time hunting you down was wasted, hmm? Worst case scenario, my son gets a pretty new pet to parade around, showing you to every single demon in existence. Your mates included."

My eyes narrow, seeking out the figure in the dark, teeth clenching in an attempt to bite my tongue. This, the doubt, is something I have battled my entire life. My parents both lacked in the human emotion department, their communication limited to instructive conversation or criticism. Their level of perfectionism is expected of me as well, something I have yet to achieve.

Taking a deep breath, I limp toward the darkness. The light slowly starts to fade the closer I get, with only the set of flaming coal eyes brightening the space ahead of me. My heart picks up its already rapid pace, beating so hard, it feels as though it is about to break through my chest, thumping against the rigid cavity with brute force.

This deep fear is an emotion I can usually redirect, slow it down enough to become pleasurable or, at the very least, tolerable. It's a tangible emotion that forces a bodily response, pushing the body to react on impulse alone. Luckily, my body's impulse is to send heat through my stomach and tingles down every single vertebrae. I itch to fight, welcoming the pain, willing it to mix with the tendrils of fear.

Every thought forces me to stand a little straighter and breathe a little deeper, the smokey air filling my lungs to capacity. I continue my descent into darkness, coming to a halt in front of the bear-sized beast. His heated coal eyes illuminate his teeth, teeth he bares at me.

My hand reaches out with more confidence than I thought I could muster in this moment, running a light touch across his heated cheek. Even sitting, the hound's eyes are level with my own.

"I am sorry he was an asshole to you," I whisper, knowing Leviathan is close enough to hear me. Not a word has been spoken since I started walking toward them, the demon waiting to see how this plays out, apparently.

The beast leans toward me, his hot breath fanning across my face. I can hear him inhaling deeply, swapping from one side of my face to the other, his snarl sending a shiver down my spine.

"You smell of my kind," he rasps in a masculine voice, a low growl rumbling in his chest. "You are a human, with the scent of a hound and a demon, and something else I can't pick. What are you?"

A smile spreads across my lips at the thought of them. Pyro, Luka, and Bale. The three men who forced their way under my skin, protecting me in an odd way. Well for now, until that scent wears off or they decide to kill me. Either way, it's helping. "A human, last I checked."

My body is pulled to the hard ground, Leviathan's boot pushing on my chest and forcing every spare breath from my lungs. I can feel my ribs begin to strain against the pressure, the pain intensifying with every second that passes. "That's enough bonding time with my demons," he snaps, his green eyes suddenly appearing in the darkness.

Even if I wanted to, I can't respond, the weight on my chest is too heavy to take even half a breath. My hands scratch at his legs, pulling and tearing the solid, unmoving mass. Seconds pass as the panic starts to take hold, tears freely flowing down my temples into my knotted hair.

"You'll get up and shut your fucking mouth. What you are about to see is where you will end up should you dare piss me off, and that would be a waste of an opportunity. This doesn't have to be horrible for you, being here with us."

His boot moves, a rush of air filling my chest painfully on the first inhale. I can sense the bruise that will form, that throbbing ache right in the middle of my chest. It will add to the array of marks sure to be scattered all over my body. My fingers trace along the bite mark on my neck, memories of last night coming back in pieces. I remember it, the feeling of Bale sinking his fangs into my flesh. That's the type of pain that has the potential to ruin me.

Slowly sitting back up, I look toward the hound sitting with his eyes pinned to the floor. His breathing is loud and focused, plumes of smoke just visible under the glow of his stare.

"Go!" he growls, his eyes cast down. Rising from the floor, I step reluctantly step toward the asshole waiting in front of me. His brow quirks, seemingly surprised by my compliance.

"Good girl. Now, come," Leviathan orders me like one would with a dog, snapping his fingers and illuminating a green-hued flame like the one he had back at the academy. As I go to follow, I take one last look at the beast, his head still hanging low, his frame hunched and defeated.

We pass multiple chain points through the hall, all adorned with gauges and black liquid. An unsettled feeling swirls deep in my gut, knowing an intense amount of pain has been felt here. The marks tell stories of beings kept against their will, more than likely by the man coaxing me forward.

"What is this place?" I breathe, not even registering that the words left my mouth until he huffs in response. I scrape my broken nails against the beam on the wall, taking in every single detail possible, just in case it's needed.

He ignores me, continuing his long strides through the hall with me struggling to keep up. There are no more hounds here, every set of bloodied chains empty on the ground.

"Do you have a plan for me? A set amount of days you will allow me to live?" I ask with genuine curiosity, attempting to keep up despite the pain flowing through me. One moment, he says he wants me alive, and the next, he has his boot cutting off my air supply. Kidnapping a whole ass human is a lot of effort to go through with no plan in place.

"Curious little thing. Didn't I ask you to follow me silently? That's twice now you have opened that mouth of yours. Unless you want to drop to your knees and make better use of it, heed my warning," he orders, not even turning to face me. Cold bastard.

We come to a set of wooden stairs leading to an iron-barred door. Each step sends sharp pain through my body from the feet up. My thighs hurt, my back aches, and my feet are starting to burn from the hot stone floor. It's not like this asshole is going to care, but the sign of weakness isn't something I really want to show him if I can avoid it.

He waves a hand over a mechanism that throws the door open with a crash. "My suggestion would be to stick close to me. Well, as close as you can manage. Do not get close to the bars. The fuckers in here bite."

I do as he says, walking a step behind him through the narrow passageway, lined on each side with thick metal bars. A foul, damp smell infiltrates my nose, drawing a sick feeling from the pit of my stomach. It smells like death, wet and curdling. The air is tainted by rancid flesh, a body left to decompose for too long before being found. Sulfur and blood.

Movement sounds in the darkness, shuffling and whispers all around us.

It smells delicious.
She's human.
I haven't smelled one of those in decades.
Just a taste, Lev, a lick.
What I would give to tear her to shreds.

The same words play on repeat, echoing through the darkness. I can hear Leviathan chuckling in front of me at the taunts, enjoying what he hears, apparently. Squinting, I try to look through the darkness to see the beings in the cages we pass, but they are all sticking to the shadows. All until we get to her.

"Don't!" he warns, his voice stern, looking at the woman holding the bars. Everyone falls silent, no more shuffling and howling, no more hushed whispers. There is nothing but silence.

Her pale face is pushed between two bars, the metal crushing her cheeks. Dainty fingers with pointed, black claws grasp the bars just underneath her face as she grins in my direction.

"She's pretty, Lev. Looks like she will tear you to pieces. It's her, isn't it? Theirs. Oh, they are going to love her!" the woman purrs, her fang cutting into her bottom lip from biting back a laugh.

She's stunning. Terrifying yet beautiful. Her skin is so light, it is almost iridescent, glowing with the flame on Lev's palm. The veins under her thin skin are dark, splitting off into beautiful patterns. Amber eyes glance over my entire body, as if she is committing every single detail to memory.

"Your bite, your mark. Can I see it?" she asks, raising onto her tiptoes to get a closer look. "It looks perfect on your skin. So perfect."

Lev grabs my wrist with his free hand, hauling me away

from the woman without another word. I trip trying to keep up with him, my two strides only just matching his one. A cackle echoes through the cages, the feminine octave sounding like the woman we just left, not like the other monsters surrounding us.

"Don't even fucking ask, or I will throw you in with her and place bets on how long you last. She's probably hungry; it's been years since she fed on a human."

She doesn't feel dangerous, not compared to whatever else is back there in the cages. Curiosity swells; I want to know more about the woman behind bars but not enough to get myself killed when I'm already on what seems to be borrowed time. He hauls me through another heavy door and up a flight of jagged stone steps. My body is going to be a wreck after this, with burns, cuts, and bruises scattered across my skin from head to toe.

Once we are at the top, it's like we are in a whole new place. Gone are the damp stones and metal chains. No more scratched floors and blood stains. Even the lighting is a few shades brighter. The floors here are a deep, dark hardwood, the smooth feeling welcome on my sore, blistered feet. Black antique chandeliers hang from the tall ceilings, illuminating the deep green damask wallpaper. From his cold reaction, this isn't a space he wants me to be in, despite him having dragged me here against my will.

If Leviathan thinks I am going to make it easy on him, he has another thing coming. If I am set to die down here in a world that isn't mine, it will be with all the wits and fight left in my broken body.

CHAPTER 3
LUKA

"You good?" I nod to Bale, checking before we take the next step. This isn't going to be easy for him, going back home, back to being around our father and surrounded by memories of a time I'm sure he wishes he could forget. But he needs Wynn back—we all need her back—and this is the only way we can manage that.

His jaw clenches, flaring at the sides as he nods, his eyes focused on the space ahead. Thick, dark blood covers his mouth and hands, but this look is nothing new for him, especially down here. Some demons find pleasure in taunting him; not many of his kind take residence in Hell for extended periods. They're welcome to a degree, but not common. Add that he is an angry little asshole with very little capacity to rein in his emotions, and it makes him an easy target. Or so they think. Most of the time, Bale comes out on top. He's underestimated, and he knows how to use that to his advantage.

The gates stand tall and imposing, thousands of flaming skulls and jagged black stones forming the archway, the low hum of hellfire vibrating at our feet. Pyro makes the first move, stepping through the iron gates as they open for us. Swirling smoke follows him with each movement, adding to how utterly terrifying his beast is. Multiple sets of glowing eyes turn our way, slinking out of the shadows and taking in the sight in front of them.

Typically, we have no issues getting in and out of Hell. The hellhounds guarding the gates rarely give us a second glance. They see souls being brought in and other supernaturals passing through, reapers and high-level demons who are tasked to something above ground. Their job is to ensure lowly demons are not able to pass through the gates, infecting the plane and risking humanity. If the gates were wide open with no one keeping track, it would be chaos. But us being the sons of Satan and a highly regarded hellhound, we should be able to come and go as needed. Emphasis on the word *should*.

The politics of this alone are going to be an absolute mess, one our father is going to have to manage at a higher level. Each ring of Hell has a leader, a prince. There are treaties in place that ensure things run smoothly down here, or as smooth as they can in a world of demons. This shit Lev has pulled, coming to Blackstone Academy and kidnapping the fated mate of heirs, it's going to cause a whole lot of trouble in the realm.

Rolling my shoulders back, I stretch out my wings, shaking them out. There will be a short time between the gates and home when they will need to be tucked in close. The tunnels from the gate's foyer to home are surprisingly narrow, considering the size of the beings tracking up and down them daily. Once we are out of there, though, I will be able to stretch them out without the fear of humans seeing me. Soaring through Hell's sky, feeling the heat from the fiery sun casting its red hue across our world, a feeling I have been craving for months.

My mind moves back to her, our little mate. The one who strolled through the Blackstone Academy without a fear in the world. She shouldn't be down here; humans can't see the gates in the first place, let alone cross them. But now that she is, once we get her back, I want to show her our world. She is beautifully curious, not shying away from the unknowns of a world she has never been exposed to, a world that should terrify her.

I imagine her thriving, exploring the depravity along with us. She will see the beauty in darkness, just like we do, even if it's only for a few days until we can figure out how to get her back out of Hell safely.

"Focus, brother. Get out of your head. Now isn't the time for a cute little daydream. We are outnumbered by those who might want to play," Bale whispers from beside me, his eyes focused on the unmoving hellhounds. His stare is terrifying, a burning intensity swirling in the bright, amber orbs surrounded by pulsing black veins. He's a vampire in his element, waiting for one to make a move, poised for carnage.

Pyro walks ahead of us, a low rumble coming from deep in his chest. His lips pull up into a snarl exposing rows of sharp canines. If he wasn't on our side, he would have me taking a few steps back. Hellhounds are one thing, but Pyro is a fucking beast.

"Do any of you have an issue letting us through?" he growls, looking at every single one of them. He shows no signs of weakness, despite standing in front of what looks like fifty-plus sets of heated coal eyes all looking at us. Pyro is different around his kind—bigger, more imposing.

One of them steps forward, bowing his head slightly as he gets closer. The hound is almost the same size as Pyro but covered in scars slashing across his fur, the black mixing with stark white. He isn't one I recognize, but they all look pretty much the same to me in their hellhound forms.

"We haven't been told not to let you in, Pyro. Archus was being his typical self; he is no considerable loss to us."

Others follow, taking slow steps in our direction, shifting the energy. One walking toward us, even with a pack of them behind him, feels a lot less threatening than fifty. Pyro stays silent, steady, watching them without moving a muscle.

Stretching out my neck from one side to the other, I try to stay as neutral as possible. The demon inside me is begging to have a little fun, waiting for one to make a move. Bale, on the other hand, is a lit fuse beside me. He's seconds away from running into the pack and slashing throats if they attempt to stop us from making it one step closer to her. To be honest, I wouldn't mind joining him.

My demon side is pent up, controlled, poised exactly how it needs to be at any given time, just as I have been taught. It would love nothing more than to reap souls, leaving trails of bodies behind in pursuit of our mate. I itch to kill something, especially if it has anything to do with her being taken from us. But it's an itch I can't scratch, not yet, not when there is this much at stake. Her.

"He has her, Pyro. He is going to want to show her off. You know him like we do. If anything, Lev would want you all back in Hell to parade his new pet under your noses," the hellhound explains before stepping aside. "Try not to get yourselves killed."

Reaching the end of the second tunnel, the smoke in the air thickens, swirling with the slight wind at the entrance. We have seen a few hounds along the way, but none have said a word to us. One look at Bale covered in their kind's blood has been enough to steer them away, their eyes on the ground.

The familiar scent floods my senses, of soft ash and

torturous emotions. I inhale deeply, sucking in as much air as my lungs allow before stretching my wings as wide as they will go. As shitty as the reason is for being back here, and the fact that our girl is in the hands of our family's enemy, I feel a sense of comfort. I wasn't built to live up there, shifted and contained. But being sent up there was an order, one I couldn't refuse, even if we had wanted to.

Our home sits on top of a mountain, right in the heart of Wrath, surrounded by a forest of charred trees, buildings and houses spread across the land. It looks very similar to Earth in some ways, just darker, more smokey. There are no green trees, nothing bright or light, not unless you are in the ring of Lust. It is a whole different space there. Otherwise, most rings of hell look similar to this: a charred landscape void of color, the emotion sucked right out of it by the hordes of demons who call this plane home.

"Alright, let's go. I will fly ahead and meet you both there," I nod as I reassuringly squeeze Bale's shoulder, noticing the rigidness in his posture. He's unlikely to speak much until he is back in his room, and what he does say will be to piss off our father. "Go straight to the pits if you need to. I can talk to Dad and fill him in."

Not waiting for a response, I spread my wings, taking off into the dark sky above them. They stand there for a moment, talking before leaving the edge of the tunnel, weaving in and out of the trees. As I course through the smoke, my body feels alive. Sweat starts to pebble along my warm skin, the temperature difference fucking with me a little. Picking up speed, I weave my way through the ashen clouds, leaving Bale and Pyro behind me. Even at top speed, they would never be able to keep up on foot anyway. It might be good bonding time for them.

This is where my body feels the freest, separated from the pressure of the world. The pressure of being Satan's son. The pressure of being an heir to a world I don't really feel part of. The façade is tiring, draining the bits of me left. Typically, I can forget it all, unable to hear anything other than the subtle roar of hellfire from beneath. No birds chirping, no sirens. No crowds cheering at sports games. Nothing.

But right now, my mind is loud and imposing, making enough noise within itself to distract from the serenity it usually feels. I'm filled with thoughts on how to infiltrate the Keep and remain within the treaty, something I am positive Bale will rip to shreds without a second thought. I ponder whether Wynn will be able to hold her own against them. Her smart mouth is likely getting her in trouble if she hasn't learned to keep herself in check, which I highly doubt she has.

I think of what Lev will do to show her off in front of the other higher level demons, the lows he will stoop to just to prove the point that he was able to take her from under us. It's all to settle an ancient score we have no part in.

The dark mansion at the center creeps up quickly, the clouds thickening as I make my approach. There are demons walking the grounds, my fathers most trusted, small specks scattered across the blackened stone. Descending quickly, I pull my wings tight against my back, landing on two feet. A plume of smoke and fog rises around me, swirling together as one.

None of his men look twice, allowing me to swing the large wooden doors open, the creak echoing through the near-empty halls. The place still feels like home, the scent, the feel. But something is different, missing. I step over the threshold, and my father calls out from his office the moment my dirty boot hits the pristine marble floor.

"I am in here. Come."

I need to go to him before the others get here, to catch him up on what's happening. If it only slightly decreases the interaction needed between him and Bale, it is worth my time and more. Heading down the hall, I can sense someone else nearby, someone or something more feminine than anyone who lives here, my father's demons included. A light giggle sounds from the office, followed by a loud, high-pitched yelp. This could be fucking interesting.

Rounding the corner, I'm greeted by my father sitting behind his desk in the large wingback chair. His fist is clenched around a gold chain, one connected to a kneeling demon. She's completely naked, her dark hair hanging like a curtain around her face, making it impossible to see who she is. Small horns curl backward through her hair, sharp and jet black. Her collar is connected to a set of cuffs on each wrist and thigh, digging into the thick flesh decadently.

"Welcome home, son. I heard the news. What do we know?" he asks, not acknowledging the demon kneeling to his left at all. She wriggles, her curved lower tummy settling on top of her thighs.

"Can we talk in front of her?" I nod in her direction, not wanting to say too much. We know next to nothing, but I am not having his toy mess with any chances we may have at getting Wynn back.

He winds the chain around his fist a few more times, tugging her roughly toward him. She looks up at me, a wide grin plastered across her face, obsidian eyes looking into mine beneath her lashes. She is beautiful, the type who would usually have my cock twitching in my jeans regardless of who was in the room, but nothing happens, not a single movement. Her white, fanged teeth rake over her plump lower lip as she stares at me, sharpened canines slicing through her flesh with ease.

"Come on, Luka. Care to join us? I am sure daddy here wouldn't mind some father-son bonding," she purrs, her forked tongue swiping out, licking the blood off her lips. The demon arches her back, pushing her ample tits out as far as she can.

"Our mate has been stolen by someone because of your history. Instead of trying to fucking find Wynn, you have this little slut in here tied in chains. You accept her trying to seduce me while she's sitting at your fucking feet?" I scowl, approaching the desk. "You're lucky it was me who got here first, not him. Between Bale and the hound, she would've been torn from cunt to throat."

Father immediately stands, his imposing height towering over her small, kneeling frame as he pulls her up by the chain, throat first. Her feet kick at the space beneath, trying to find solid ground with no luck.

"If you sat with your pretty little mouth shut to start with, you could have been the one to tell him what he needs to know. Out. I will deal with you later!" he snarls, dropping the demon to her feet with the chain wrapped tightly around her neck. She struggles past me, her thighs still bound to her wrists, forcing her to waddle as she walks out.

Closing the door, I cross the room and sit in one of the lounge chairs in the corner, eyeing my father. He shifts from one emotion to another extremely quickly, from anger to stone-cold and stoic within seconds. Still standing at his desk, he places both hands firmly on the wood as he stares at the empty doorway.

"I don't know how many times I have told you not to challenge me. Whether it is behind closed doors or in front of other demons, you are to fall in line. Do I make myself clear? I already have one son who is a ready fuse, waiting to explode on anyone who crosses paths with him. I would prefer to not have two," Father orders, his gaze lowering to the drawers in the desk.

My jaw tenses as I bite back my words, knowing now isn't

the time. I need to be the one to take the brunt of this, his harshness. The orders. The lambasting. This needs to be me.

"The succubus. She heard whispers about your little mate. It would explain another reason Lev has chosen now to stake his claim."

My father's hands drop, opening the lower drawer and pulling out a black crystal glass with a bottle of amber liquid. It isn't like he can get drunk, but he likes to collect old whiskey and scotch from above ground. He drinks it when he needs something else to focus on. Situations like this.

"It looks like there may be more than three of you, son. This is about to get extremely messy, and I am going to need you to listen carefully. Rash decisions will end in war, her being the pawn in the middle." A look of concern comes over him as he lifts the glass to his lips, downing the scotch without a wince. "One wrong move, and you will never see her again."

CHAPTER 4
WYNN

Heated hands encircle my thin wrists, pulling me along too quickly to take in anything around me. My feet stumble, clambering up the large wooden staircase and down toward a dark hallway. Memories flood my mind of my room at the academy, being separated from the world down a dark hall feeling extremely familiar. Lev stops us in front of a door, pulling out an old-style key from his pocket and forcing it into the brass lock. The metal-on-metal sound slices through the tense silence as he unlocks the door with a loud click.

His hand moves from my wrist to my lower back, pushing me through the open door into a room that takes me by complete surprise. I was expecting a damp cell, maybe an empty room with a mattress in the corner and a bucket to pee in if I was lucky—dark and gloomy, not at all comfortable. I can't help the smile that creeps across my face at the stunning space, and I take in every detail as though the demon isn't even there.

"I trust this is to your taste, then?" he queries, leaning against the door frame. Considering the rush he seems to have been in to get me in here, he's acting much too casual. He takes his time examining my body, taking in every mark, every flaw. There's no heat behind his perusal, his disgust abundantly clear in the way he pulls his lip up, peering down at me as though I'm no more than dirt under his expensive, patent leather shoe.

"Minutes ago, I couldn't get you to shut the fuck up, and now, you suddenly lose your ability to speak?" he asks abruptly, frustrated by my lack of response.

"Sorry. You threatened to throw me to my knees and make use of my mouth if I spoke again, remember? I would much prefer to keep your dick away from my mouth," I laugh, turning around and limping toward the giant, four-poster bed. I trace my fingers along the soft comforter, my jagged nails snagging the fine fibers, small pulls forming in the fabric.

He takes measured steps; three of his long strides is all it takes to reach me on the other side of the room. The demon looks down at me with his cruel green eyes, a smirk tipping the corner of his lips. Without a word, he wraps his slender fingers around my throat and tilts my chin up with his thumb.

"Your smart mouth will be the death of you, human. Don't let it be the thing that winds you back in those cells. I took you through the dungeons for a reason: to show you the alternative should you decide to be a defiant little cunt."

Lev's grip on my throat intensifies, radiating pain through my neck. I attempt to suck in a breath, but he stops me in my tracks. He squeezes until swirls of black haze my vision and the panic creeps in. My heart rate climbs, the pulse thrumming through his bruising fingertips. Black and green blurs into one, my vision slowly slipping with every second that passes.

"I brought you here, and I can just as easily discard you. You are nothing to me, a pawn. Step out of line, and you will be thrown back down there with her. Only for you to be ripped to shreds by her, it would be utterly devastating. Devastating and beautiful."

He lifts me by the throat as if my body weighs no more than a feather, tossing me onto the plush bed sheets. Moments pass, maybe hours. I can't really tell by the time consciousness slips back in, the room still spinning behind spots of black. It feels empty in here now, silent, Lev's presence long gone.

Taking the moment of peace, I look around the stunning space. It's beautiful, like a bedroom torn from a gothic castle, with its large wooden bed and mirrored vanity. The timber is well worn and looks almost scorched, with black filling all the knots and grains of the wood.

I rise from the bed, a little unsteady on my feet, and pad over to the only other door in the room, praying for a bathroom. Despite this feeling like a room from a castle plucked from the olden days, I would prefer to not pee in a pot under the bed. I am wildly desperate for a shower, the soot and dirt clinging to my skin, clogging every pore. Just the thought of hot water running over my muscles elicits an unexpected moan. A shower bringing pleasure—that's a new one.

Opening the door, my breath is stolen from my chest as I take in the space. A massive, clawfoot bath sits in the middle of the room, floor to ceiling windows along the far wall. The shower off to the side is stocked with bottles and vials that look like they belong in a potion class in a movie, not in a shower. They're all strange shapes and sizes, not a single one with a label. Roulette with hellish soaps sounds like fun.

Taking curious steps to the window, I get my first real look of Hell, and it's even more beautiful than I thought it would be. When you think of Hell, you think of fire, little red sprites with horns and tails, black skies, a whole lot of death. I expect to see people being torn limb from limb, terrifying creatures stalking around. That is the Hell depicted in books and movies. But this? This leaves me breathless. Much like the three beings from this space that walked into my life and completely took over, landing me here in the first place.

Demons, vampires, and hellhounds are not supposed to be attractive, dripping in sin and darkness. They're supposed to be terrifying and horrible, scary creatures who make you run in fear for your life.

My hand splays out over the warm glass as I lean in closer to get a better look at the new world below me. There's heavy smoke swirling with the wind, but the landscape looks like a printer has run out of ink. Shades of black and gray cover each surface. It's void of any brightness or color other than the slight red hue from the moon. There's no greenery, just blackened branches and dark houses scattered amongst the hills. There are specks, some smaller than others, moving around out there. Closer to the window, there is a tall, iron-spiked fence wrapping around the castle I find myself in, two large hellhounds fighting just below.

Aware of the fact that my body is on complete display this close to the window, I flick the light switch off. This allows just enough light to see but not enough to draw attention. Stepping into the shower on the other side of the room, I finally feel like I can take a deep breath. My pulse rises as the scorching water stings my skin, redness spreading at every impact point. Searching through the glass vials, I choose one that faintly smells of jasmine before washing my entire body two times over.

Gray bubbles swirl down the drain, the soot and debris finally lifting from my skin. It feels like heaven, an odd feeling, considering I am in the depths of Hell. Between what I saw out of the window and the walk up to here, there isn't a doubt in my mind Leviathan is telling the truth. He has brought me to Hell. Now, I just need to fucking survive.

Out of the corner of my eye, I see movement along the

window. Darkness flows across the bathroom as something blocks the already-dull light. The water droplets on the shower door make the figure a little hard to see, but it's large, whatever it is.

Immediately jumping out of the shower, I slip a little, reaching for one of the towels to the side. Bright green eyes penetrate the darkness, not unlike Lev's, but this isn't him. This being has horns adorning both sides at the top of their head, with a wingspan that reaches from one side of the glass to the other.

My pulse rises, eyes darting around for something to defend myself. Anything. I draw blanks, my eyes now pinned to whoever is on the other side of the glass. He grins, the white fanged teeth standing out in the darkness, a sinister smirk directed right at me. The shadows hide his finer features, but there is no mistaking he's enjoying this. Looking in on the newest animal in the zoo. That's what I would look like from out there.

"Did you get the show you wanted, huh?" I snarl, wrapping the oddly soft towel tightly around my body. He probably can't hear me through the glass and stone, but at least it makes me feel a tiny bit better. I'm in danger down here; it would be idiotic of me to not realize that. My life quite literally hangs in the balance, at the mercy of beings much more powerful than me. That doesn't mean I'm about to completely fold, though.

The asshole laughs, his whole body jolting while he relishes in my little tantrum. He stares for a few tense moments before dropping from the window, disappearing as if he was never there. Slowly walking over, I look down to see if I can catch him, but there is no sign of him at all. Nothing. Even the hellhounds from earlier are missing, leaving not a single soul within eyesight.

Searching through the drawers leaves me completely emptyhanded, a complete and utter waste of time. No clothes, nothing. Not a shred of fabric other than the sheets on the bed and the towels on the rack. It seems like the space belonged to someone feminine at some point, with the intricate filigree on the wallpaper and the deep jade green curtains adorning each window. They bunch elegantly on the floor—flooring with not even a single speck of dust.

My fingers glide along the soft sheets of the bed. I take some pleasure in the fact that I may have no clothes to sleep in, but at least the bed is nice. This was not at all what I was expecting. There's the stone and the fire, the darkness and the smoke. These things align with my thoughts of Hell. Soft silk sheets and soap that smells of jasmine, not so much.

Before settling into the bed, I cross the room to the mirrored dresser and drag it in front of the door with the last shred of energy my body possesses. Not that it will do all that much, but if someone happens to open the door through the night, at least I will hear them with the wood scraping the floor. My muscles pulse under the pressure, burning through my arms and thighs, but I manage. The shower did a little for the soreness wracking my body, each movement draining the fight left in me by the second.

Settling into the welcoming bed, I stretch my worn body out, the overused muscles screaming at the release, the silence, the comfort, the solitude. All of it on a typical day would feel amazing, my ultimate space. But today, it lets the thoughts creep in, thoughts of what in the world has happened over the last 48 hours. Even I can admit it's overwhelming.

With the time to breathe, it allows my brain to let the walls down, even just a little. To think about the fact that mere days ago, I had no idea that the paranormal really existed. I had always hoped, wished the creatures I read about or watched were real. Fast forward a few days, and not only have I learned they are real, but somehow, I am linked with them on a level beyond my wildest nightmares.

CHAPTER 5
BALE

Need thrums through my veins, pulling me in the opposite direction of where we are going. I've fed on her. Fucked her. Claimed her. She wears my mark on her collarbone, one they would have seen by now, considering she was stark fucking naked when Lev stole her. Taken from right under our noses.

It's as though my entire body is being pulled in her direction ever so slightly, the small movement causing intense pain. It's worse than anything I have experienced before, and my life has been filled with torturous experiences. It intensified when I walked out of the room earlier tonight, a light hum delicately dancing along my skin. It was there when she first arrived, the need flowing through each vein, muscle, and bone, but it was nothing like this. Nothing compared to her.

No. This is pain. *Hunger.* Within days, this girl has gotten under my skin and forced my body to crave hers. My fangs ache, throbbing through the gums into my jaw. I am more than aware of it being a death wish to walk into Envy, demanding they hand her over to us. Despite what Pyro thinks, I am not the mindless moron he believes me to be. But if we don't get to her soon, the small amount of control I do have will slip, regardless of the consequences.

Pyro's emotions are more controlled, but they are just as deadly as mine. Growing up as a vampire in a world filled with demons taught me a thing or two about emotions, how to read heartbeats and facial expressions. I can't do so as accurately as a demon, but I can still read emotion in some capacity. With his reputation down here in Hell as one of the most brutal enforcers, as well as his darker emotions he attempts to hide, we are more alike than I wish to admit.

If Luka and Pyro felt even a small amount of the pain, just a little, they would understand my need. Giving in, tasting her, claiming her—it was all a risk, one I planned to avoid. But here we fucking are, about to step foot into my own personal hell to get her back. I'm plagued with not only hatred from my father for things I can't change, but now with an intense thirst and need for a woman in the grasp of his enemy.

Sharp claws dig into my destroyed palms rhythmically, the memory of her resting heartbeat still lingering in my mind enough to replicate. Blood, pain, and the memory of her helps. Just, but it helps.

Pyro and I sprint to my father's home without uttering a single word. The thundering footsteps of the bear-like hound are the only thing breaking the silence. Luka lands well ahead, his black wings falling from the sky with enough speed to wreck himself if he doesn't nail the landing. He's reckless when he flies, using it as an escape from the lives we are both forced to live.

Approaching the tall, imposing metal gates, we are forced to wait for the demon on guard to let us both in. They take their sweet time, clearly in no hurry. Pyro takes the moment to lean in, pushing his shoulder into mine with a sharpened grin.

"What do you think, Fangs? Want to go down and fight it out? I know I sure as fuck could use it," he laughs, shaking his body out beside me. His eyes remain pinned to the gate in front of us, watching for movement. Two of my father's demons stroll up side by side, cold, expressionless faces watching us. That's until one cracks a smirk. I don't have the patience to deal with these two pieces of shit today.

"Ahh, the reject son returns with his new pet dog. How fucking sweet," Elias laughs, tilting his horned head to the side. His molten eyes are alight, enjoying the moment a little too much for my liking. Nothing changes down here, these idiots included. He nudges Kai in the ribs, motioning his head in our direction. "Look how cute you are, all covered in blood as usual, Bale. Daddy is going to go fucking ballistic when you tramp that through his precious mansion. He won't be able to get the stench of mutt blood out for weeks."

Kai reluctantly opens the gates, staring at the pair of us with a shit-eating grin plastered across his face, one I would give anything to wipe from his face more permanently. Taking a deep breath, I walk forward, slamming my shoulder into Elias as hard as possible on the way, forcing him to the ground. Before I even register it, Pyro's jaw is around Kai's arm, blood dripping onto the hard stone beneath us. The hellhound grins, looking up at me before clamping down harder and severing Kai's limb. The thud of the forearm hitting the ground is like music to my fucking ears.

I place my boot on Elias' throat, pressing firmly as his hands grip my calves. He thrashes beneath my hold, the movement barely shifting mine. The feeling of his life force slipping away is a rush, sure, but it's nothing compared to the addictive sensation of her blood flowing freely through my veins or her soft warm skin beneath my hands. Today isn't the day to fuck with me, not with her missing.

Lifting my boot, I slam it back down with my entire body, the crunch of his bones echoing through my ears. Feeling his death beneath me does little to calm my instincts, too quick and clean. It's going to need to be a hell of a lot more than a quick death—something slower, the feeling of blood rushing through my fingers or a heart starting to struggle under the pressure.

Kai scurries off, the blood from where his arm used to be creating a steady flow of crimson in his path. He isn't so brazen without his friend here, not speaking a word as he runs around the corner of the house and out of sight. He's likely running to my father to tell him what happened. Serves him right for hiring pieces of shit to guard his precious house.

"I know you say hellhounds taste bad, Bale, but that demon was foul." Pyro wipes his mouth on his front leg, his lip pulled up in disgust. He isn't wrong; demon blood isn't great. It lacks flavor of any kind, about as bland as they come. They can keep my kind alive, but not thriving in any way. A means to an end, nothing more and nothing less.

We make our way to the pits, the sound of screams and flesh being beaten hitting our ears before we enter the vast space. The pits are a place of comfort for me. Not many people are game enough to get into the ring with me these days, though.

When I was younger, we had a running list of opponents. Demons put their hands up left and right to spar with Satan's son. It was a chance to boast about their strength should they succeed, even though I was a literal child. Pent up with rage and strength beyond their own, but still a child.

As I got older, stronger, more bloodthirsty, that's when the volunteers dropped. Luka indulged me from time to time, needing to let off steam of his own, usually after a run in with our dear father. When he's all pent up and angry, letting his demon side out to play...fuck, could he fight then. He has much more restraint than me, but when that restraint snaps, he's just as deadly, if not more so.

Passing the rings cordoned off by thick chains, we find one

unoccupied toward the middle of the dark room. As we step through the chains, Pyro shifts into his human form, the smoke engulfing him completely. He has to be kidding.

"I am not fighting you naked, for fuck's sake, Pyro!" I growl, looking around to see if there are any of the usual demons walking around. "Someone get the beast a pair of fucking shorts."

He's in front of me, completely unashamed about the fact that he is standing there with his dick out. His arms are crossed over his chest, a wide grin flashing at my obvious annoyance. Minutes tick by, the wails and screams now silent. Everyone around has stopped, their eyes pinned to the two of us.

A demon I have never seen walks up to the ring, throwing in a black pair of shorts and a tank for Pyro before stepping back a few steps, leaning himself against the next set of chains.

Pyro stretches his neck from one side to the other, cracking bones sound from each side. There's a glint in his eyes, a fire dancing behind his black pupils, a hunger that matches my own, the craving of violence.

Out of the corner of my eye, I see Luka and our father walk into the pits, deep in hushed conversation. I try to zone in on what they're saying, but I'm pulled out of it with a snarl seconds before a hand wraps around my throat, burning my flesh instantly. *Again*.

Standing my ground, I step closer, fangs descending through my pained gums. My vampire side has been itching to come out to play, *properly* play. Not a quick death, no neck snaps, no tearing out hearts and ripping them to shreds. No, this will be different. This time, I will be able to bring someone to the very brink, the slowed heartbeat, eyes blown wide. Moments passing where he won't know if I am going to finish him off or let him heal enough for another round.

Not that he will meet a true death by my hand, knowing

he is her mate as well. Regardless of whether their bond is in place, it would cause her immense pain. Not the kind that would make her pussy drenched, but the kind that would damage her soul permanently. I don't particularly like having to share her with anyone other than Luka, but now is Pyro's chance to prove where his loyalties lie.

"Focus on me and how you would love nothing more than to beat the ever-loving shit out of me. Leave them to talk about whatever they need to. Luka will tell you later anyway," Pyro snaps, his face inches from mine. His heart rate speeds up, the organ now rapidly thrashing against his ribcage. I wouldn't be surprised if that bruises.

Flexing my claws, I push my hand toward his lower ribs, slicing through the thin skin at his side. Blood gushes through the webs between my fingers, the drips echoing in the otherwise silent room. Forcing his body to step back, my hand now nicely inside his side. I lean down until my fangs graze his ear.

"Don't say I didn't warn you, Balto. You want to fucking fight—let's fight."

He flashes a sharp-toothed grin, not flinching at the fact that my bare hand is beneath his skin. "I have always wanted to come face to face with you. At least now, we can't actually kill each other," he huffs, stepping back swiftly. Removing his hand from my throat, he takes a layer of skin with him, and fresh air floods my raw flesh, a war between extremes of fire and ice.

Nothing we do to each other down here will permanently injure the other, not unless we want to. He knows that as well as I do. So this intense pain, the skin removal and the claws playing blender in his side, it's all temporary. It's a feeling I embrace, and for the first time in a very long time, I may have met my match.

The rest of the room blurs as the two of us circle the mat.

Fists fly, connecting with flesh and bone. Blood splatters, mixing both his and mine beneath us. We fight for what could be minutes or hours, taking moments to regain our breath between each blow, neither one of us backing down. My body is broken, exhausted, begging for a reprieve to breathe properly.

"*Enough*!" my father roars from somewhere in the room. His voice is unmistakable. My mouth fills with blood from a split in my lip, forcing me to spit it out to the side. The splatter blends with the drenched stone beneath us.

"You have had your fun, son. Come on. Clean yourselves up and meet me in my office in ten minutes." With that, he turns, disappearing into the house without a second glance. Such a caring father.

The two of us stand there, both heaving deep, heavy breaths. Sweat drips from Pyro's brow, the usual intense arch now furrowed. He wanted this fight as much as I did, needing to feel that pain and concentration only fighting could give.

My finger swipes along my split lip, collecting the blood escaping the gash before I run my tongue along the remnants. The things I would give to be able to tear Pyro's head straight from his body. The way my claws crave to slice out his tongue for being inside her, not once but twice... But I won't.

CHAPTER 6
WYNN

My body stirs, slowly moving and stretching out under the soft sheets. Part of me hopes it was all a very realistic nightmare, not something I would call uncommon for me. But the other part knows as soon as I open my eyes, reality will come crashing back to smack me in the face at full force.

Each flex of my muscles sends pain pulsing through my body, the same feeling as the day after a workout. It's pain that is nothing more than an ache while dormant, though still intense with any kind of movement. It's not like I can just ask for an Advil and some bath salts; Lev doesn't seem like he would give a shit about someone being in pain. Quite the opposite.

My stomach rumbles and growls, muffled by the layers of blankets I'm under, acid bubbling at the surface. Rummaging through the room last night proved pointless; I found no weapons or clothing, nothing in the way of food. A small grace is, the water in the bathroom seems to be like back home somehow, safe to drink. However, water won't keep me going for long.

Opening my eyes, a squeal escapes my mouth at what's in the corner of the room opposite the bed. The being from the window last night sits on the lounge, his fanged grin once again alight in the darkness. I scramble, reaching for the sheets and pulling them to my chest, my back against the headboard.

"What, didn't get enough of a show last night? Now you're watching me while I sleep?" I ask, wondering how long he has been in here. I have yet to get a full view of him, but he engulfs the vast space. Large, black wings are held out to each side, the tips resting on the ground. From the outline, they look a hell of a lot like Luka's did that night, but this sure as shit isn't him.

The being shifts, his leg stretching a little farther as he seems to settle back into the chair. The movement on leather is the only sound filtering past my heavy breaths. Blood begins to rush to my ears, the warm hum of my increasing heartbeat louder and louder by the second.

My eyes dart to the door, assessing the mirrored dresser in front of it. There are no signs of movement at all. Snapping my gaze over to the window, I see one of them is cracked, letting a soft, subtle breeze flow through the curtains. He must have come through there.

"You climbed through a window to watch me sleep? Surely, I'm not that fucking interesting. You're in Hell. Go tear some guts out of someone or something and leave me in peace!" I snarl, leaving him completely unphased.

The being laughs, the low octave of his voice smooth, soothing. Deep breaths pull from my lungs, calming the race of my heart with every exhale. I shouldn't be feeling this calm, not with him in here. It's almost as though a switch is flipped deep inside me, switching my body from one emotion to the next with no rhyme or reason.

Within moments, my body is back to where it was—racing heart and itchy skin. Beads of cool sweat slowly drip down my spine, my body incredibly aware of every sensation. Heat pools in my lower stomach, moving its way through my core, where it tightens, pulsing through the warmth.

"What the actual fuck is happening?"

I'm now drenched, my skin soaking the sheets while I watch the asshole cautiously, his chuckle at my expense catching me off guard. He rises from the chair, his height guiding my eyes as he dodges the chandelier and walks confidently toward the bed. Black wings scrape along the floor behind him, the sound near deafening in the silence.

I don't know what they put in the water down here, or what sort of magic shit they have been drinking, but once again, I am faced with a man who looks like he was carved by the gods themselves. His dark hair is messy, slicked back, with a few tendrils falling into his eyes and horns that look they belong on a demonic farm animal. He's dressed in all black, his button-up shirt undone at the top, giving an air of decadence that fits with the room I was pushed into.

His green eyes blaze with a mix of humor and hunger, clearly appreciating my panic. Sadistic fucking asshole. The closer he gets, the clearer his features become, a silver scar splitting through his lips. Scars, horns, and wings. *What in the walking wet dream is happening? Did I actually die and go to heaven in the night?*

My vision blurs with tears, my body completely overwhelmed with the constant back and forth of emotions. For someone who tries their best to steer clear of emotions that serve no purpose, this is pure and utter torture. I am usually able to control my emotions well, steeling myself when needed, finding pleasure in fear and pain, willing my body to feel what life has to offer, rather than accepting the blank slate my parents forced upon me.

When I was first faced with the twins and Pyro, I felt a pull, one I wanted to fight, but an instant connection that couldn't be explained or ignored. Butterflies swirled in my stomach and my heart raced. The physical desire to be close to them, to touch them, was overwhelming, something that had never happened to me before with anyone.

The pull is there with this being too, that I can't deny. For all I know, it could be a power of his kind or something—luring people in, lulling them into a false sense of security before killing them and harvesting their insides. I add that to the list of shit I don't know about the creatures down here.

Hot tears stream down my cheeks one after the other, the sound of them hitting the sheets filtering through the tense silence. He sits in front of my gathered legs, leaning in until his face is level with my own. Both wings curl around me, trapping me with no way out. Even if I could get away, the doors are locked, and I am on at least the third floor in a realm I know nothing about. It would be foolish of me to run.

His emerald eyes curiously follow the tears from my eyes to my chin. The air feels unexplainably heavy between us, a familiar feeling swirling through my body. He leans in close, his heated breath fanning across my wet cheek. I try to ease myself away, to put some distance between us, but he stops me in my tracks. Firm hands grasp both sides of my face, his fingers digging into my cheeks with bruising force.

He extends his tongue, long and forked at the end, dragging it from my jaw to my eye and clearing the salty tears on one side. His eyes roll back at the taste, a low rumble sounding from deep in his chest as his head drops back. All my eyes can focus on is his corded neck, the way the veins are dark under his skin as though it is close to translucent, how his Adam's apple moves when he swallows, a movement that is completely natural but feels incredibly masculine.

"You're even better than I thought, little human, with tears much sweeter than I am used to." He smiles, returning his gaze to me, a devilish smirk crossing his stunning features.

He looks familiar in a way that doesn't sit right. Surely, I would remember seeing someone who looks like him, all dark and broody, with horns and wings. He isn't the type you would forget.

"Oh, so you do speak, huh? I am going to repeat my question for you nice and slow. Why were you in here, watching me sleep?" I snap, a little of the fire returning to my veins. My hands grip the sheets tighter, white-knuckling the edges, pulling them as high up my chest as I possibly can.

His fingers dig into the flesh of my cheeks, eyes focused on the points of pressure. Redness is sure to be blooming across my skin, the white halo around where the pads of his fingers meet my face. My focus shifts, only slightly, but enough for a short reprieve from the overwhelming feeling of being in the same space as this man, whoever he is.

"Pretty sassy for a human whose life depends on me. What did you think would happen while you slept in one of Hell's castles? That you would have sweet dreams and be blessed with the smell of bacon when you woke up?" he asks.

Removing his hands from me, he sits back and stares at me, his brow cocked. I peer around his wings, once again looking at the dresser. It doesn't look like much, even I can admit that, but I did my best with what was available. Which, in here, is sweet fuck all.

"Baby, you think a dresser will keep demons out? That they wouldn't slip in here and fuck you raw just to get the feeling of a live cunt wrapped around their cocks? Hellhounds would thrive in that pretty little mind of yours, haunting your nightmares as you sleep."

I stare at him blankly, the words caught on the end of my tongue. As much as I want to fight him, my knowledge of this place is limited. Nowhere near enough to keep me alive for long.

"As pleasing as the mental image of demons taking their

turn with you is, we have shit to do. Come on, little human," he orders, getting up and moving the dresser like it weighs absolutely nothing.

"Unless you are hiding a change of clothes in your pocket, I'm not going anywhere," I throw back, grateful for the distance between us, giving me space to breathe. Standing, I wrap the soft sheet around my body and tuck the corner in around the top edge, creating an oversized wrap.

He leans against the wall next to the door, arms folded across his broad chest. His eyes rake up and down my body without shame, taking in every single inch he can see with a heavy focus.

"Do I look like a wizard or something to you? Where would I possibly be keeping clothes?" He gestures, throwing his arms out and turning in a circle, as if to show he is carrying nothing.

"Well, if you took away the whole wing and horn thing, added some glasses and a scar, you would be pretty fucking close, if I am being honest." I choke back a laugh, my teeth biting into my lower lip to stop any more words from falling out.

He walks toward me, ripping the sheet from my body and dropping it to the ground. His wings disappear from his back on the way over, not in any way changing the demonic appearance of this man. Even without them, he's menacing, the attitude mixed with the horns. My hands scramble to cover myself, one arm across my chest and the other between my thighs.

Unbuttoning his shirt, he shrugs it off his broad shoulders and holds it out, waiting for me to take it. I hesitate, wondering what the catch is. He's a demon who was watching me shower, watching me sleep, and has quite literally licked the tears from my cheeks. Tears that I still don't quite understand fully but believe he had something to do with. Why would he now be showing a shred of mercy?

"Take it or leave it. I have seen your delectable body a few times now, little human. I don't mind forcing you down there stark naked if it means I can drink you in while I show you around."

Admitting some defeat, I rip the shirt from his hands and storm to the bathroom, slamming the door behind me. I can hear the low chuckle from the other room, the springs of the bed compressing as he sits. My entire body is littered with bruises and cuts. Purple and blue dot my skin, red fingerprints marring my cheeks from his brutal hold.

His black shirt is soft, wrapping me in his strong scent. That scent that comes to mind when you think of a men's cologne,rich and masculine. *Expensive*. The type that lingers long after the person has walked past. His shirt hits just above my knee, with the sleeves dangling from the ends of my fingers. I roll them a few times before splashing cool water on my face at the basin. I need to wake the fuck up for whatever it is I am about to walk into.

CHAPTER 7
LUKA

It's absolutely no use attempting to talk to Bale after a fight, especially when he teetered on the brink of death with his worthy adversary close behind him. The fight had settled the bickering between them, more on Bale's side than Pyro's. Seeing them in that chained ring, covered head to toe in each other's blood, it was easy to see they were both in their element. If only it was that easy to settle the demon inside me, rattling at my ribcage to get out and hunt its mate down.

My father is practically useless. He wants to ensure we will stick by the treaty that keeps the rings in order while he digs with his 'sources' to find us an in. He believes, having met Wynn and witnessed her fire, that she will be fine so long as she doesn't piss Lev off endlessly. For Satan, the literal Prince of Wrath, he is incredibly sensible. Not often does he utilize the unhinged, extreme anger he is known for. It's there, simmering under the surface, but it rarely comes out to play how it used to, or so I have heard.

My jaw tightens, needing to pull a deep breath and center myself before leaving. How in the world can he sit in his mansion while his sons' fated mate is out there, locked up in the Keep with his lifelong enemy and his beast of a son, is completely beyond me.

Fury licks at my skin, needing an escape that doesn't involve going up against someone with zero hope of winning. If this was *his* mate, he would be moving mountains to find her, tearing the rings apart one by one to get to her, but *we* have to follow a treaty and stay in line.

If a single hair on her pretty little head is hurt, I will gladly go against his wishes. I'll join forces with Bale, and likely Pyro if I'm being honest. Both would love nothing more than to storm the Keep and return with our fated, as well as the skins of every single hellhound that crosses our path.

Extending my wings, I plunge into the deep darkness of Hell's night. The sky is practically black with thick smoke covering the full moon. It will take a while to get to the very cusp of the ring, sitting right on the very edge of our border to meet with a few old friends.

It has been almost a year since I saw Alexander and Alexis, the vampire twins. They're old, having been in Hell for hundreds of years on and off and existing on Earth's plane for almost as long before that. Not many of their kind stay down here for extended periods, preferring the open hunting grounds of the humans above. But these two, they are too sinister for the human world, only going up a few times a year for a feast.

Our father tried to introduce Bale to them a handful of times in an attempt to get him around his own kind, but even when we were kids, he was a solitary asshole. True to their nature, I guess, but Alexander and Alexis are a wealth of knowledge we could use to our advantage.

So here I am, being assaulted with the scent of sweat, blood, and sex in the underground club owned by the twins. I haven't even landed before the scent smacks me in the face, my nose twitching the closer I get. The whole area is dimly lit, with a small crowd lining up at the deep crimson doors.

Their club is like a smaller scale version of Blackstone Gates. It's all gothic and moody, with pointed arch windows and tall towers. Music thumps from inside, the beat heavy. When I land right out front, the two burly demons on security nod, opening the door without question. A few screams and insults are hurled from the line, but I don't give a single flying fuck. What use is it having the pressure of the underworld on your shoulders if there are no perks, like direct entry to things?

I attempt to weave through the crowds, tucking my wings flat against my back but not shifting and removing them completely. Down here, it's a sign of power, not something to hide or shift away. Now more than ever, I need the demons here to know we are not to be fucked with, because every single one of them could be a key to getting our girl back safely. The bass of the music vibrates my body, forcing a shiver up my spine before shaking out the tips of my wings.

Hands reach out as I walk through, grappling with my arms and wings, trying to pull me aside. My teeth gnaw at the inside of my cheeks, my hands balled into tight fists, trying not lash out and deck the touchy assholes. Typically, I can keep my cool, shine the megawatt smile, and flirt with anything that breathes to keep the peace. But today isn't the fucking day for this, not with her missing.

Each hand burns my skin, their touch painful, as if my body is repelling them, knowing it has found its mate. This is new. A female demon blocks my path, her arms crossed over her chest, pushing her tits up toward her chin. She wears scraps of leather and white material that drape from her body in random places, leaving very little to the imagination. As she steps closer, her tail drags up my jean-clad leg, the point tearing a thin line in the fabric.

"Get the fuck out of my way!" I growl, grabbing her

shoulders to push her aside. She plants her feet harder, resisting my shove. Her eyes light up like the lava pits in Hell's core, brightly glowing as she drinks me in. Of course she fucking likes it.

"Come on, baby. It's not every day we see one of the royals down here, slumming it in a club. Let me take care of you. There's a spare booth just over there. I bet you can scent my pussy this close. It's been dripping since you walked through the doors. One look has it leaking down my fucking thighs," she purrs, reaching her head forward and flicking her long, forked tongue across my pulse point.

My hand moves to her delicate little throat, gripping tightly as I lift her off the floor. I can hear the club quieting around me, the whispers flowing from one demon to the next.

Usually, it's his fucked up twin doing this shit.
What's he going to do?
It's his dad's land. He's gonna kill her.
Maybe he'll fuck her first.
I heard his mate is a vision. He won't stoop that low with her alive.

"What part of no did you not understand?" I sneer, my teeth clenched. She picked the wrong demon on the wrong night to fuck with. The pent-up frustration bubbles at the surface of my control. I can feel it slipping, disappearing into darkness and welcoming my demon side out to play. Not just the wings or the tail, not the height or the charm—no, it's the downright viciousness begging to pop her joints from the sockets, shoving the flesh-covered bones down her throat until she chokes on herself with me watching.

"Unless you are a fucking moron living under a rock, you know I have met my mate. What in the world would make you think I would want to fuck trash like you in a club?"

I bring her face close to mine, her soft panting almost making me retch. Each breath she pulls makes my hand tighten until her spine crunches beneath my fingers. I watch as her emotions switch from lust to intense fear, and I siphon what I can from her. May as well make her last moments on this plane useful before she's sent to rot with the rest of the damned souls.

She thrashes in my hold, dragging her long nails along my forearm until lines of beaded crimson form on my skin. Kicking her legs out, she fights hard against me, but I don't move an inch, reveling in her pain. Just as the life in her eyes starts to dull, I snake my tail out behind me, settling it between her thighs. There's a small moment of surprise that flashes across her face, false hope that this was just some intense foreplay, the needy bitch tilting her hips to grind onto the razor sharp tip.

"You wanted to be touched by royals? Consider your last wish granted," I snarl, digging the edge of my tail into her slit, slicing the demon from clit to throat in one swipe. Blood pours from the clean cut, her clothes hanging haphazardly from her thrashing body.

Her eyes blow wide, knowing she is about to meet her fate. Tears stream down her flushed cheeks like an open faucet, mixing with the blood on my arms that has already begun to dry. If not her, it would have been the next one who came crawling out of the darkness. This way, it sets the standard. I'm out.

I lock my fingers in her blonde hair, gripping tightly as I wrench it to the side with all my strength. Her vertebrae pops instantly, the light in her eyes sparking until the dull hue of death sweeps over the red orbs. I drop her limp body to the ground, swiping my tail on a patch of clean fabric clinging to her side.

The once-handsy crowd parts, allowing me to walk through without so much as a breath in my direction. I can see them, Alexander and Alexis, standing up in their VIP area.

They're looking down at the body with fanged grins, Alexis nudging her twin with her elbow.

Alexander shifts his focus to me, the asshole flipping me the bird before descending into the darkness, hand in hand with his sister. I shake my head, a silent laugh clenching my stomach as I climb the velvet stairs to meet them. My shoes stick to the drenched fabric with each step, making me shiver. The amount of alcohol, blood, and other bodily fluids sticking to the floor in this place is disgusting, but fitting.

We are in Hell, I get it. There are very few rules outside the treaty. It's a sinner's playground, the place to be if you are the type to partake in debauchery and death. These two, however, they kick things up a notch, flaunting their dysfunctional relationship to the masses, their fangs sinking into each other every chance they get.

The two bouncers part as I reach the top, speaking into their headpiece that I'm approaching. Music still thumps loudly, vibrating the floor beneath me with each bass drop, but the sound is now much more muffled in this confined space. The stench of sweat and sex is muted up here, still present but dampened.

Their VIP area is enclosed. Large, cathedral-style windows show the club below, a door opening to a large balcony, the same one they watched me from moments ago. This space reminds me a lot of some of the areas of the academy, only the club has more black and drips with the decadence you would expect from a vampire-owned establishment.

"We've missed you, blondie. It's been, what? Twelve months since we laid eyes on your pretty lil face? Want a celebratory drink? This is fresh, coming from above just today," Alexis coos from behind their personal bar. Her decanter clinks with the glass as she pours. Thick, crimson liquid spills over the top, running across her pale fingers and onto the counter, leaving a puddle.

"Not that. How in the world you drink it like that, I have no fucking idea. Is it not better from the source? You wouldn't need to go up there long to find people willing to deal with you," I respond, grabbing myself a crystal glass from the shelf. The club is familiar for me, an escape, one I frequented before I left for Blackstone.

"I hear you found the girl. Your beloved." Alexander grins, walking toward me with open arms, drawing me into a tight embrace. It constricts my chest, the breath in my lungs struggling to escape. He releases his grasp, holding me at arm's length to get a proper look. With them, it feels different. Unlike the rest of Hell's population, who look at me and see my father, these two see me. I consider them family.

My empty glass is filled with a clear liquid as Alexander pulls me toward the large, leather chesterfield sofa. His amber eyes focus on mine, eagerly awaiting a response. Alex's emotions are level, curious, as if he genuinely wants to know more. Leaning back, I swallow a large mouthful of the vodka, embracing the burn flowing down my throat into my chest. "I sure fucking did, Alex. I sure fucking did."

Alexis joins us, sitting on Alexander's lap with her arm draped around his neck, her stained fingers grasping the blood-filled glass. His hand moves to her bare thigh, drawing what looks to be an A with his lengthened claw and creating little blood tracks. He kisses the crook of her neck before returning his focus back to me.

"Tell us about her."

Images of Wynn flood my mind, mixing beautifully with the lust pouring from every being in this club. The pairing goes straight to my cock, forcing it to twitch beneath my zipper, its metal teeth digging into my length. My teeth bite into the flesh of my cheek, attempting to calm it the fuck down. Unlike my mate, or my brother, for that matter, pain doesn't get me off. Inflicting, yes. Experiencing, no.

"She's feisty. Very fucking feisty," I laugh, remembering how she walked into class bloodied just days ago, the dead raccoon dangling from her perfectly manicured fingers. I didn't want to get addicted, to be consumed by her, but she made that impossible without even knowing. "We tried to prank her a little on the first night at Blackstone. She walked in with the dead animal in her hands, asking if we wanted her to cut it in half so we could share."

The twins chuckle, Alexis leaning in closer, a grin plastered across her features. They are textbook vampires, the kind humans depict in their literature, with ink black hair and pale, almost translucent skin. Their features are regal, angular.

"More, I want to know more. She's human, no? Oh, I can't wait to meet her, Luka. I promise not to hurt her," Alexis urges, her excitement taking over. If there was anyone down here I would trust to keep Wynn safe, it would be these two, and they know it. She takes a drink from her glass, closing her eyes the moment the blood hits her lips.

"She is. Completely human, not a hint of anything supernatural or otherworldly in her. I mean, she has a presence, but it's her. Not what she is, but who. It is hard to explain." I mull over the words, coming up completely blank. The truth is, a lot of it isn't explainable. She's unique in so many ways, made perfectly to fit with us, all three of us. Maybe four, but now isn't the time.

"She's your mate, Luka. If she treats you how you deserve and doesn't reject the bond, we are on her side too. What happened to her? How did Lev manage to take her? We have heard whispers, you know how it is down here," Alexander asks, leaning in to take a drink from the glass in Alexis' hand.

"We were outside the room, trying to straighten a few things out, when we heard commotion. Ww walked in to find Lev nearly pushing her through a green mist. One can only assume it lead to the Keep, but we don't really know for sure."

My jaw clenches, mind whirring with images of his hand on her flesh. The need to strip his bones bare grows each moment I am separated from her.

"What can we do to help? We know a lot of demons and hellhounds, ones who frequent the club. We can see if we can get some information from the inside, even if it is to know she is safe," Alexis offers, genuine concern flowing through her body. I siphon what I can, the emotion stronger than anything else in this place.

"I would forever be in your debt."

CHAPTER 8
AXTON

Defiance has never looked so delicious. The feisty human walks out of the ensuite completely drenched in my scent, my shirt clinging to her curves. It looks huge on her, hitting just above the knee, her hips grazing the sides. My scent mixed with hers makes my eyes roll back, a low growl rumbling from deep in my chest. Her presence draws out the most primal parts of me, coaxing them out to dance with her darkness—a darkness I can't fucking wait to explore.

My father has been vague, talking about the fates for weeks now, how an old hag he had imprisoned has foretold something about a human girl, one who is fated to royals. My knowledge of her kind is limited, having only interacted with them a handful of times, but they don't seem like they could survive the wrath of a lust-filled demon, let alone multiple. Their breakable bodies are all delicate and soft. One wrong move, and they're dead.

Seeing her so close, tasting the salty tears mixed with the notes of her skin, fuck. She looks up at me, her tiny frame shadowed by mine, curiosity in place of fear. The girl has been stripped bare, walked through my father's prisons and thrown into a room in the depths of Hell itself. After a singular night of watching her, syphoning her natural emotions as she slept, I can tell she is going to brighten this dark fucking abyss I call home, a responsive plaything all to myself.

The Keep sucks demons dry, utilizing their talents until they are no longer of use. Father sometimes keeps them for toys, down in his little creature zoo below, the place he sends the ones too useful to kill. But if they don't live up to his standards, they are sent deep into the pits, where the lost souls wither away until there is simply nothing left.

"Ready to see your new home?" I ask, biting back a laugh at the eye roll that follows. She's a dramatic little human. Her hands meet the curve of her waist as she cranes her head forward a touch. Dark, knotted hair falls over her shoulders, brushing lightly across the black material. I can't wait to have the fabric back in my hands; the scents of the two of us combined has my dick twitching, aching for her already. Wynn makes no attempt to hide her gaze, her eyes lowering to my belt buckle and back up again.

"Do I really have much of a choice?" she snaps back, her dark, angular brow lifting at me. She walks closer until she's standing right beside me in the doorway, the proximity doing nothing to calm the storm she created by merely existing. Not bothering to resist the urge to touch her, my hand engulfs the side of her delicate neck, tilting her head up to meet my stare. Humans don't usually do it for me, meat suits with mundane views of the world, but not her. Limited interaction or not, she has crawled under my skin, making her mark on the darkness they call a soul.

"Not really, no. Your kind withers to ashes if they are not physically fed, and I haven't had my fill of you yet."

"What do you mean, fill of me? Is that easy enough for you to answer?" she asks, taunting me, staring right at me with not a single shred of fear. My frame is at least a few feet taller than hers, adorned with wings and fucking horns. "You stalk me for one single night and feel like you're entitled to something?"

"My father collected you as somewhat of a gift, to see if his old hag was onto something when she mentioned the sons of princes—emphasis on the multiples, " I explain, guiding her out of the room and into the hall. There should be something for her to eat down in the kitchen if my father has done his due diligence. Surely, he has at a bare minimum gotten her some food—or maybe he plans for her to be dead sooner rather than later, a thought that leaves a sour taste in my mouth and an unsettled feeling in my chest.

Her eyes widen as she takes in the halls outside her suite, almost every inch of it covered in a rare piece of art or sculpture. My father's obsession with having what the rest of the princes do plagues him, whether that be sculptures and pretty things, relationships, or really anything to do with their lives, which is where this human of mine comes in. Mine—it has a nice ring to it.

Delicate fingers wrap around my elbow, the broken edges of her nails digging into the sensitive flesh of my inner arm. The most trusted hellhounds can stay in the Keep, roaming as they wish so long as they do my father's bidding when he calls for it. Which is why Silas is walking in our direction, a toothy grin spreading across his lips. He is one of the oldest of his kind, covered in scars, an absolute beast.

"Mmmm, I thought I could smell something sweet." He licks his lips, tipping his nose into the air and inhaling deeply as he steps closer to Wynn. Instinctively, I grab her hand and pull her behind me, forcing her to duck under my wing. The hem of my shirt lifts enough for Silas to get an eyeful, exposing her completely. An unexpected wave of possessiveness has me growling, taking a step in his direction, my body poised for his carnage if needed.

What is it about this girl that has me ready to tear the eyes out of the hellhound I have known for my entire life, whatever the consequences? Looks like Miah will be getting a little trip above to dress this morsel clawing at my back, because fuck if I am having the hellhounds seeing all of her.

"Manhandle me again, asshole, and see what happens," she bites behind me. Her hands push firmly into the back of my ribs, the broken nails biting into my skin. "Exposing myself to an oversized dog in Hell wasn't on my fucking bingo card for today."

As much as her fire excites me, now isn't the time, not with him circling her like he would innocent prey, waiting for the moment to strike. Any other hellhound, and I wouldn't be concerned. Most cower at the very sight of me purely because of the treatment my father has forced on them. Assumptions are made that because I am his born son, I am the same. Cruel, unreasonable, wicked to my very core.

Not Silas, though. He doesn't act without my father's explicit direction, so he has been sent as a warning. A play of control, to show me she may have been given to me as part of his little show, but he pulls the strings.

"C'mon, Ax, don't hide her away. She's a fucking treat. It's not every day we get one of these toys, not ones this pretty. I like 'em feisty; I reckon she would be a screamer." He stalks closer, beads of drool dripping from his mouth onto the floor. I turn, curling my wings around her enough that he would only be able to see up to mid-thigh if he's lucky.

Fear starts to weep from her pores, sweet and sinful, pure —like a drug for a demon, one I could see myself getting addicted to rather quickly. Silas whines, his eyes closing as he too feels the shift in emotions from deep within her. Concentrating just as I had earlier, my control starts to spread through every fiber of her consciousness. It slowly puts out the raging wildfire of fear, replacing it with contentment, something he will find no joy in.

It's a power I heard about a while ago, a rare gift very few demons possess, a dormant ability that can spark when you encounter your fated mate. The pull I felt to the girl earlier had me curious, my father's musings running through my mind. Yet another indicator this fragile little being has storms in store for her. Being able to get the twins and Pyro on one page is one thing, but we were raised to hate each other.

Silas continues his slow stalk down the hall, his head hung low, eyes pinned to her thighs until he passes the two of us. "Keep her close, Ax. Wouldn't want her falling into the wrong hands, now, would you? Not all of us are able to resist, no matter the orders. That pretty cunt of hers is a fucking beacon."

"Eyes, ears, and everything else off her, do you understand? Tell them all, each and every mutt down in those fucking caves. She's a gift, my gift. Sniff in her direction again, and I will personally be the one to end the infamous Silas, stripping your skin from your flesh and feeding it to the lesser demons for breakfast. Now fuck off!" I snarl, listening closely to the shallow breaths behind me.

Unfurling my wings as he turns a corner, she bursts out, her chest heaving with each breath. No longer under my control, her fury flies free the moment I stop. The brightest of blue eyes scan the room, settling on me once she sees Silas is no longer here. Fuck, she's cute when she's mad, so small and harmless.

"Come, little human, before the shred of control I have decides to disappear. The fear, anger, and lust is a heady mix for a demon. So unless you would like to skip lunch and take a run through the woods with me, keep yourself in check." My hand drifts to the small of her back, lightly ushering her toward the kitchen. If the girl has any hope of surviving life down here, she will need to adapt quickly.

Feeling this way about another being is foreign to me. Fondness of any form. Sure, there have been moments when Miah has pulled some emotion from me—that drive to protect her from the wrath of my father is there, the banter. We have a friendship of sorts, built on the foundation of self-preservation and being able to survive living close to the man who sired me. But this little human sparks something else entirely, a more primal need, something I very much want to indulge.

Reaching the kitchen on the lower floor, she stops in the doorway, scanning the entire room in confusion. Her teeth bite her plump lower lip, the blush skin turning white along each impact point. Surely, she had a kitchen up there; this can't be new to her. Not that I was told a lot about her, other than the fates spouting shit to do with her producing heirs who threaten the very existence of Hell.

"Coffee?" I question, walking over to the drip machine on the black marble counter. She stays silent, confusion settling across her features. Grabbing two glass mugs, I pour the rich liquid into both, sipping on one while I walk back over to her.

My father chooses this moment to enter the room, dressed in his usual dark green suit and black shirt, wings sitting proudly at his back. He silently sits at the head of the table, unfolding the newspaper under his arm and giving it a light shake to straighten out the pages.

"What the fuck is all of this?" she asks. Her brows cinch together as her hand waves around the room. She points directly at certain places around the kitchen, the coffee in her hand included.

My father looks up at her from his paper, staring at the wall ahead of him for a moment before looking toward the two of us. Her human hearing wouldn't be able to hear the curse words flowing from his clenched teeth, but I sure as fuck can.

"Not only are you delicate, you're stupid too. The fates are really making this a lot harder for me to believe." He gestures for Wynn to come closer in his usual demeaning tone. My sharpened teeth bite the flesh of my cheek, an attempt to tamper the response lingering on the end of my tongue. I would love nothing more than to react, to bite back, shielding her from him, but my father is the prince of Envy for a reason.

What I wouldn't do to be able to kill the piece of shit who raised me, to tear him from his gold-adorned pedestal and feed him limb by limb to the scum he has banished to the deep depths. But doing so means I, being the one and only heir, the sole demon with his blood thrumming through my veins, would have to take over.

The thought alone would have him tearing at my skin, ensuring permanent scars so I *remember my sins.* For a man who has been in Hell since its very formation, he is wildly rigid. The thick scar down my lip throbs at the memory, the intense pain trying to mend itself together from the inside out, only to leave a big enough crack for a scar. One of his proudest moments, I'm sure.

She gulps down some of the hot coffee, her eyes rolling to the back of her head for a split second, breathing out a low moan. The sound mixed with her reaction goes straight to my dick; it's an inopportune time for it to be thickening beneath my slacks. Good to note—don't give her coffee unless seated.

"Do that with your eyes again, little human, I liked it. I can't fucking wait until it's my cock forcing your eyes to roll back," I whisper in her ear before walking over to the table, my wingtip brushing along her upper thigh on my way past. She swats her free hand at it, connecting hard with her knuckles along one of the ridges.

"Fat chance of that ever happening. I am literally a

prisoner. He kidnapped me and tossed me in here, and you don't seem like you're going to help me get out. So tell me, why do you think that thing is coming anywhere near me?" She halts halfway to the table to stare at me with mock fury. The girl is conflicted, warring with herself. Her emotions mix into one, lust and longing with a sprinkle of anger.

"Your sense of self-importance is admirable for a human, I will give you that. If my son wants you, Wynn, he has you. It's sweet you think you have a choice in these things. You are in Hell now, girl; the rules of humanity don't apply down here. The main ruling body here is me within my jurisdiction," my father responds to her, frustration lacing his tone. I am surprised he is explaining anything to her, to be honest. "Now, sit down and eat. You can either do it yourself, or I will have one of the doctors put a tube up your nose and force it in."

She follows begrudgingly, sitting to my side but pulling her chair hard up against the corner of the table. Extending my wing, I hook the tip around the leg of her chair and pull her flush against my own. Reaching down to her bare thigh, I dig my fingers into her skin, the pressure making her squeak. It's not like she can run all that far, but now I have her, I'm not taking any chances. She isn't safe within these walls, not with my father and Silas stalking in the shadows.

"Now that we have that sorted, have you never seen a kitchen before?" I ask, genuinely curious. "I haven't been up there much, but I thought they were a pretty common thing in houses. You seem shocked."

She dramatically takes a deep breath, steeling herself. She's curious and frustrated, all mixed into one cute little package. Her hand attempts and fails to rip my fingers from her flesh, those jagged nails tearing into the skin on top of my hands, shallow pools of blood gathering between the raised tendons. My grip on her doesn't waiver in the slightest; if anything, my fingers tighten with the pain.

"Of course I have seen a fucking kitchen, asshole. What I'm confused about is why in the world demons in Hell need one?" she bites back, looking between both my father and me. "Do you even eat? How the fuck does he have a newspaper?"

"We are not here to give you a lesson on our kind. Axton, we have business to attend to. Some food for thought, though, if your brain has the capacity for that. Where do you think all the demons living down here came from? The architects with a penchant for blood or the scholars who liked to sleep with their students for grades? Demons are not just cold blooded killers, Wynn; many souls are too tainted for the world above." Father rises from his chair, nodding toward the door for me to leave with him. He leaves no space for argument. "Don't make me drag you in front of your pretty little pet now, Axton."

My jaw tightens, as does my grip on her skin. Anger pulses through my fingertips, and she takes the brunt of it. Her legs shift in response, rubbing together with my hand partially caught in the middle. The heat between her thighs reaches me, tempting me to lift my hand even just a little. The girl isn't wearing any panties; one movement is all it would take to feel her bare pussy on my fingers.

Just as my hand connects with her core, she's hauled up by the throat and thrown to the ground, scrambling to cover herself, her wide eyes looking between the two of us. I jump to stand between them, but my father pulls at my wing, throwing me into the wall behind him with little to no effort. This fucking cunt.

"Stay there, Axton, or so help me Lucifer, I will take her for myself," he orders, taking measured steps to where she sits, kneeling so he's face to face with her. With the anger rolling off her, I'm surprised she hasn't slapped him. There must be some self-preservation in there somewhere, thank fuck. I want to be able to tell her to just cool it and he will leave her alone, that if she just takes his anger, he will spare her.

This shit isn't new to me in the slightest. Surges of anger with usually only me to take it out on. As much as I would like to rip the assholes head off and toss him into a pool of lava for even looking at the girl, that's a death sentence for both of us. His strength and power would take ten of me to beat or more.

"What the fuck did I do? You told me to eat, so I ate. If you wanted me to move, you could have just told me," she snaps at him, her fire breaking through.

He wraps his hand around her throat, squeezing enough that she starts to panic. I step closer to them, but he senses me, turning his focus to me while she clings to the last shreds of consciousness. His mask has slipped, the cool composure he wears like a disguise dropping to reveal the demon I know, the one more terrifying than Leviathan the Prince of Hell.

"You will both need to learn exactly who is in control here. I see the defiance on your face, Axton, the moment of hesitation to do as I ask. Let me be clear, she is here because of me and can be removed whenever and however I see fit."

She claws at his arms, frantic to suck in a breath, tears streaming down both sides of her red-tinted cheeks. They're tears I want to taste, to clean from her skin to remove the tainted emotions of my father's presence. Her heart races, trying with everything it can to keep her going. He has to stop, or this was all for nothing.

CHAPTER 9
PYRO

It has been over a week now, and still nothing. No contact, no leads on an in. Nothing. We expected Lev to make a show of his prize, to dress her up and parade her in front of the higher-level demons for a show of power, all the while knowing full well we can't take her back without bloodshed. It's bloodshed that will destroy the treaty that has been in place since the very beginning of Hell.

Every single source I reach out to has been banished from the Keep, hellhounds ordered to stay outside the gates. There are a few still roaming around inside from what they have said, but none who would have anything to do with me. Even if I begged. Silas and Miah are devoted to Lev and his son, Axton, following them around like lost puppies since their very existence. Several others have been stationed within the Keep, guarding it from us I am assuming.

Whatever game Lev's playing, he seems to be fucking winning so far. It takes all of me not to storm in there and rip her from his grasp, my hellhound side all but whining every time I shift, needing to be closer to its mate. We are one, not two separate entities, but sometimes, it feels as though my most primal side overpowers rational thought. It's lucky all the hounds I have met with have been reasonably safe, or there would be total and utter carnage to deal with.

Wrapping the dark towel around my waist, I trace my fingers along the risen slice of skin below my ribs. Bale did a number on it, slowing the healing right down to a snail's pace. He treated my insides like they were in a blender, slicing his claws through every organ he had access to. I've struggled to sit since, the bend in the skin excruciating, sharp pains rippling through my side.

The twins and their father encouraged me to stay here so we could strike quickly when the time came. Well, Luka and his father had, anyway. Bale retreated straight after the fight, barely coming out of his wing since. They put me in one of the guest rooms on the twins' floor, the space backing onto Bale's wing on one side, Luka's on the other.

As I walk out of the ensuite, a loud smash sounds from Bale's side, like wood splintering hard against the floor. I can feel his anger through the walls, emotion flowing strongly. It's palpable, feeding the hunger deep down that has been craving more than the demons down here can provide. He's intense at the best of times, but the bloodlust has to be driving him to insanity at this point, the raw craving for his mate a primal reaction.

"*Fuck!*" he yells as he hurls another item, this time at a window. Glass shatters, echoing through the space. His boots fall heavy across the floor, the anger intensifying by the second. The vampire would have no qualms tearing me to shreds if he found out I was siphoning his emotions without permission. My moral code may exist, but I'm a demon at my core, and the only emotions stronger than anger this visceral are lust and fear.

Walking to the bed, I sit down, resting my back against a cushion of the headboard. My head falls against the wood as I allow myself a moment to soak in the slight high from drawing in such intense emotion. Closing my eyes, images of Wynn flow freely through my mind. The way she whines when she is about to come, the faces she pulls, her venom-laced tone with no regard for the true danger she is in around our kinds... Fuck, even the vision of her thighs spread open that night, her pussy leaking with Bale's release comes to me unbidden.

The anger from Bale's room shifts; it's still angry, but there is an edge. A hint of lust spreads rather quickly, creating an addictive mix that has my dick twitching beneath the towel, my knot pulsing at the base. I look down, debating if it's worth potentially getting my spine torn out through my throat if he ever finds out.

His lust wins the battle of wills, now flowing headily through the space. If anyone else was in the house, they would know. There has been no movement or voices, Satan rarely home and Luka usually out with his little vampire friends. Any demon within the walls of the mansion would be able to feel the surge; surely, he knows this. Maybe he just doesn't give a shit.

I move the edge of the towel to the side, allowing my cock to spring free from its confines. The lighting reflects off each barbell adorning the underside, stopping at my engorged knot. It's visibly pulsing, aching, craving a release.

Since tasting her the night she bonded with at least one of the twins, the need has been intense, even painful at times. My body physically needs to be close to hers, preferably deep inside her, marking up her body, chasing her, breeding the absolute fuck out of her.

Chills spread across my heated skin, small bumps forming across every exposed inch. A carnal growl rips through the walls, and the small whisper of control I have slips completely, disappearing into thin air without a trace.

Rolling my tongue around my mouth, I spit into my palm, spreading the warmth down my length. My teeth grind as I glide my firmly-fisted hand up and down my cock, pulling at each barbell with my palm. The enlarged knot at the base begins to swell from my touch, indicating there is no turning back now. Pain to that level isn't worth it.

The thoughts of her staring into my eyes as the twins fucked her relentlessly in the woods that night plays on repeat. The raw hunger in her gaze—she knew I was watching, and she welcomed it, hellhound form and all. It has me questioning whether she will like it, seeing my dick in my more primal form. The size alone scares even an experienced being of the same kind, but she would revel in it. Too bad it has the potential to tear her in two with the tip piercing through her mouth if I were to lose control.

My hips buck up with force, slamming my cock through my clenched fist, the intense lust fueling my movements. Licking my other hand, I wrap it around my knot, chasing the building pleasure. It takes mere minutes before my entire cock is throbbing in my palms, beads of precum dripping through my fingers.

Bale curses in the room beside me, his need to take the edge off things mirroring my own. His low moans are barely audible even with my hearing, but they are certainly there, building and building until he snarls through his release, his heavy footsteps thumping across the floor moments before a door slams.

Picking up the pace, I force my hand to grip tighter, the pressure easing the closer I get to the sensitive tip. Warmth gathers at the base of my cock, forcing my stomach to tighten and my balls to tense. I'm so close, my breathing ragged, chasing every bit of pleasure the moment has to give.

I run my thumb over the drenched head, engulfing it completely with my palm before one last glide from tip to base. An intense orgasm rolls over my body, ropes of cum covering my stomach. My teeth bite into my lower lip to hold back the groan threatening to escape, careful enough for the asshole next door to not hear a peep. The muscles along my stomach tense, cum dripping from one ridge to the next, running down my side and onto the towel below me.

Using the towel to clean up the mess, I throw on a pair of ripped black jeans and a tee before lacing up my combat boots. My lungs need to breathe, the air in here thick and rich with emotion.

Exiting the room, I follow the sweeping staircase to the lower ground and sneak out the back door. My body slides down the manor wall until my ass hits the stone ground, my arms resting lightly on my knees. The demons around here are unlikely to kill me, but I am in no state to be fighting them off. Siphoning emotion to that degree is like taking a relaxant. My muscles feel at ease, loose on my bones. The slight tingle slowly spreads across my heated skin. If that's what it feels like getting myself off while feeding on someone, I can only imagine what it will feel like being wrapped in my little mate while doing it.

A sense of power spreads through my senses, an alertness piquing that someone is approaching well before they are in view. My shadows start to flow out, the energy to shift not quite there yet. They can't do much to protect me, but aided by my fists, I should be fine against a run-of-the-mill demon while I am under the influence of heavy emotion like this.

Satan rounds the corner, looking behind him before approaching me. Out of respect, I rise to my feet, bowing my head slightly in his direction. The demon exudes an intense amount of strength and authority without any effort at all, demanding the respect his level of being has.

"Ahh, Pyro, just the hellhound I was looking for. Let's take a walk," he instructs, leading the way with sure, determined strides. Dark circles have settled beneath his eyes, and his platinum blond hair is unusually messy. Other than the handful of times I have seen Satan in a fight, he is always one of the more poised princes. A surprising turn of events, considering he is the Prince of Wrath.

I follow along beside him, a step to the left, weaving amongst the tall, charred tree trunks until he comes to a stop. It's odd for him to want to speak with me alone, without the other two, or more likely one alongside me. Before all of this, he utilized my skills on occasion, so we are familiar, but not enough to be having small chit-chat in the woods alone.

"I know this has to be rough for you, for all of you. As someone who was separated from their mate abruptly, I understand the longing on a level the twins have yet to recognize. This little firecracker, however, has not one, but three of you prepped and ready to hunt her down to the ends of this plane and the next."

He looks past me, checking to make sure no one has followed us out here. Bale is unlikely to be around him willingly, and his guards know their place well enough to not follow unless instructed.

"It's getting harder by the second to not storm the Keep and rip her from Lev's cold, dead hands," I respond through gritted teeth. The fire pulses through my veins at the mere thought of tearing out his throat and stealing her back.

"I know. Which is why I am tasking you with something. See, I know him. The sources that told me about the fates are from Lev's compound. He knew before any of us. When I found out it had to do with my sons, I infiltrated the Keep with one of my own. He can't get her out, not without help—which is where you come in. Hellhounds meeting is a hell of a lot less conspicuous than if me or the twins were to meet up with him. I need you to head to a club downtown and meet with him tonight for updates," he orders, taking a deep, heady breath as he finishes.

"Consider it done."

CHAPTER 10
WYNN

Considering I am apparently in the deep depths of Hell, *the* Hell, my days are becoming somewhat normal. There is no doubt I am a prisoner in the Keep, unable to run away or escape. After my near-death run in with Lev the day after he hauled me through the mist, I have managed to not piss him off too much.

They have let me have free rein of the Keep, so long as either Axton or Miah is with me. Whether it's for my own safety or to keep tabs on my whereabouts, I have no idea. Miah pads into the room in hellhound form, her white fur a stark difference to the darkness surrounding us here. It smokes like the other hellhounds, billowing out more with each step or movement. But that's where the similarities end.

Where most hellhounds I have seen have red or shades of orange burning in their eyes, Miah has icy light blue. When my eyes first met hers on my first day, the questions came tumbling out of my mouth. She explained a little about the process that hellhounds usually go through to become what they are and that she was born. When she shifted into a white hellhound, however, she was traded and sold, ending up here, a rarity amongst the masses.

"You were out like a light last night, not a single dream or nightmare," she confirms, her muzzle pulling up into a smile. Axton has asked for her to stay outside the room at night. She's there in case any of the hellhounds in the Keep attempt to nightmare walk, the same as Pyro had. Since arriving down here, they have mostly stopped, only a few short, random dreams flitting in and out of my sleep.

"You don't have to sleep on the floor out there every night. I am fine. What's the worst they could even do? They can't kill me in real life when they are in my nightmares, right?"

"Wynn, these hellhounds are not like the one you have as a mate. Even he is deadly as fuck, but he would want to protect you because you are his. These ones Lev has in the keep, they will make all your nightmares a reality, and not the good kind," she huffs, her head hanging low.

We have spent a lot of time together over the last few days. Miah threads as much information about the beings here as she can into conversations. I'm not used to having interactions like this with people, preferring to steer clear if possible on every occasion. But she is working her way through my wall, the one that took all my years to build and fortified with shitty experiences and horrible interactions. Somehow, she is slowly cracking through the solid foundations.

"Come, let's go to the library. I have pulled out a few books on fated mates and demonology for you. They don't seem to have a single thing on vamps here, which is kind of weird, but I can tell you most of what you need to know there too." She throws her snout at the doorway. "Lev is out, and Axton won't be back for a few hours. The only other hound here is someone I think you may want to meet again."

Curious, I walk over to her, pulling the hem of the t-shirt Axton threw at me this morning when I woke. It smells richly of him, wrapping me in his scent. At first, it pissed me off, taking the clothes purely because there was no other choice, but it's growing on me, grinding down my resolve since his father tried to kill me, filling in the blanks and keeping me as safe as he could.

"Who is it? I only know of you and Pyro, who I very much doubt they are letting within these walls." I try to not get my hopes up, my breath catching at the thought. I can't properly explain the emotion of missing someone you hardly know. I've had minimal interaction with all three of them, and yet they plague my thoughts, my body needing to be closer to theirs. It's a connection I have no idea how to wrap my head around. Like a marionette on a string, something invisible coaxes me toward them.

I follow her down the quiet hallway, we make our way to the library that has been my comfort the last few days. It's filled with floor-to-ceiling bookcases, complete with one of those fancy sliding ladders. This place puts my cube units to shame, although they are certainly missing the kinds of books I typically like to read. No monster porn in sight. A shame, really, It's a fun way to pass the time, that's for sure.

"Not your fated mate, no. If he steps foot over these treaty lines, he will be as good as dead. Same for the Blackstone boys." Her head drops even lower than before—not the news she wants to be giving.

"And if I step foot outside of this place, I'm as good as dead too. Cute. I fucking love my life."

As much as it hasn't been completely horrible here, this won't last. Lev may have been vague with his plans for me, but living out my days in a castle is likely not what's in store.

"Wynn, I know it isn't great here. You miss them. I see it in you, that longing lingering under every emotion you have. You have demons within these walls who would sacrifice themselves to keep you alive and as comfortable as we can.

This hellhound is one of them." She nods ahead to a man I hadn't noticed in the darkened corner of the library. He leans against one of the desks, dressed in distressed denim jeans and a black tee, looking me up and down with red-hued eyes. He seems oddly familiar, but from where, I have no idea.

"Wynn, this is Cassius. You met him on your first night. He was chained in the lower levels of the Keep," Miah introduces the man as she walks across the room to greet him. "He poses no threat to you; if anything, quite the opposite. Having more of us on your side within these walls will help."

I walk closer to the pair, taking in as many details as I can. The man looks much less imposing than the beast, his dark hair hanging low in front of his eyes. She's right to a degree about having support in the Keep being beneficial. I have only met one other hellhound over the last few days, one who looked like he wanted to devour me whole, and not in a good way. Axton kindly told he me would be a regular within the walls and to stick with Miah if I have a shred of self-preservation. Which, for the moment, is still intact.

"Why would you want to be a glorified babysitter for the newest pet in the zoo here, Cassius? Isn't there more fun shit to do down here? Slice and maim, bathe in the blood of your enemies?"

He huffs out a laugh, shaking his head, his whole body lifting with each breath. The sound is warming, bringing a very genuine smile to my face. Miah is the first to speak, looking directly at me.

"Babysitter? Here I was, thinking we were slowly becoming friends," she taunts, a sly grin spreads across her lips, showcasing her sharp canines. The feeling is a little foreign to me, sitting strangely in my mind.

Being brought up how I was, with emotionally void parents and morbid interests, making friends or wanting to be around people isn't a familiar practice. Spending the majority of your life being rejected by peers and looked down upon by anyone else kind of does that to a person. Silence and solitude are my friends, the space where I can be completely myself without a single shred of judgment or prejudice.

"The only ones I want to slice and maim would get me killed for good this time. You, a puny little human, showed kindness to a beast in his worst state, brimming with rage and anger, a fucking animal." He seems angry, his eyes swirling with shades of orange and red like pools of lava. "But you looked past it, concern flooded your emotions. I don't think you understand just how rare that is, how rare you are."

His words render me speechless, not a single retort lingering on the end of my tongue. No sass or snide comments, nothing. Blank. My heartbeat starts to rise, thumping loudly in my chest as the pair look at me. Their eyes flit from each other to mine and back again. No one has ever spoken about me in that way, and I am entirely unsure of how to process it.

My entire body is covered in sweat, heat radiating intensely from behind me. The soft sheets are drenched, sticking to my slick skin. I try to shift, pulling the wet sheets away, when an arm snakes around my middle, drawing me closer to the source of heat. My heart rate spikes, the panic starting to take over as I attempt to catch a glimpse of them.

"Morning, little human," Axton rasps, his voice deep and husky. Goosebumps skate along my exposed skin, acutely aware of the fact that my naked body is curled against the demon, his cock hardening against my ass. There's a hint of relief, knowing it's him, the demon who has made it his mission to get under my skin since I stepped foot in his home.

I try to move away, failing miserably as he shifts his body, his hand now gripping my throat and his huge body hovering over me. Sleepy emerald eyes bore into mine as a sleepy smirk spreads across his face.

"Get the fuck off me!" I snap through clenched teeth, frustrated. His grip tightens in response, the motion spreading heat straight to my core. He's enjoying the fight, his cock stone against the apex of my thighs, creating friction. My hips instinctively buck, chasing something they certainly shouldn't be. Fuck.

"Mmm, you sure that's what you want?" He ghosts his lips along my exposed neck. "Because your scent tells me the opposite. Lust so thick, it can't be masked and a pussy begging to be filled."

He grinds his cock into my heat to make his point, and wetness seeps through the material of his boxer shorts. "I can't wait to smell like you when we go on our little adventure today. As much as I would love to get myself lost in that pretty cunt of yours, we have somewhere to be."

Axton gets up off the bed, picking up his shirt from yesterday off the floor and offering it to me. He has done this every day, giving me the shirt he wore the day before. "This will aid the demons in knowing you're mine. Wear it."

"We have gone over this, asshole. I'm not yours. Give me the fucking shirt," I deadpan, rolling my eyes. "Where are we going exactly? And are button-ups with no shoes or panties in the dress code?"

His hands reach up to my chin, grasping firmly with his thumb and forefinger and shaking my head from side to side teasingly. "So cute for something so sassy. Miah brought clothes for you the first day you were here; I just prefer you wrapped in my scent. Plus, it means there are fewer layers when you get a little scared, and it turns you on."

He makes a point of telling me. in great detail, every single time that happens, which I hate to admit is often. Since the night in the woods, the same night I was taken, my body has been hungry, craving a release in a way it hasn't before. It's a deep-seated need I can't even fill myself because there is someone with me at all times.

Here, there are no blades to help, so my nails are jagged and broken. But even so, it would never compare to the pure euphoria I felt being in between the twins while Pyro watched. My mind wanders to that exact moment, watching the drool drip from Pyro's jowl as he watched intensely. Those fire-lit eyes watching over every bloodied, naked inch of me.

My core clenches at the thought, yet again. That fire burns deep in my lower stomach, stoked by thoughts of them, the way they made my body feel like it was more alive than it had ever been.

"There you go again, Wynn. How many times do I have to tell you, my patience only goes so far? I'm a demon; self-control is not my forte. You can't just go getting all hot and fucking bothered in your own little mind. It takes every single fiber in me not to rip these sheets off and sink myself into you. You're fucking dripping." He moans at the end of his outburst, inhaling deeply. "Get in the shower before I take it back and fuck you raw, whether you agree or not."

His words do nothing but intensify the heat, and my body reacts on pure need alone. That sort of comment should scare me coming from a being like him, but it doesn't. If anything, it makes me want to test him more, just to see how far I can push before he snaps.

CHAPTER 11
WYNN

I find Axton and Miah in the corner of the room, deep in hushed conversation. She shakes her head, her long, ice-white hair swaying over her shoulders. This is the first time I have seen her in her human form, and she's breathtaking.

She's slightly shorter than me, with luscious curves, dressed in a white latex dress clinging to her body like a second skin. Her long, pointed white nails bite into the shiny material, surprising me that they haven't punctured through with how hard she grips her hips. He said something to piss her off.

"You cannot be fucking serious, Ax. You would be putting her at risk!" she snarls, pulling her lip up to showcase a row of sharp canines. Even in her human-like form, they are gnarly, sharp enough to rip off a limb if needed. She's a weapon in her own right.

"While I appreciate how passionate you are about my mate, should we not let her choose? I think she would rather like it down there, where the real fun shit happens."

Mate. That four-letter word has been hanging in limbo.

He insinuates it, commenting on his ability to alter my emotions at will as being a sign there's something in store for us. The math is starting to add up, but it doesn't make it any easier knowing I am a whole part of this thing. I'm having so much trouble grasping it—how me, the heir to nothing but a business dealing in dead bodies and funerals, could be linked to otherworldly beings is beyond me. It makes no sense at all.

"Depends; what do you mean by fun shit?" I throw back, my mind a fog of whirring thoughts. These walls have become a bit of a safety, despite the threats inside them. It's known territory here, the hounds familiar and kind. Well, most of them. This could be my only chance at getting out, at seeing the twins and Pyro again. If they are even looking for me.

"I have ordered you a gift, but it is made by a lesser demon, one sent to the pits long ago," he explains. His intense stare switches between the hellhound and me. "What do you say, little human? Want to see where the demons go to let loose?"

"What he's failing to tell you is that it is very fucking dangerous down there. Your scent is strong and enticing. They will come for you. This asshole can't keep you safe on his own." Miah shoulders Axton firmly as she makes her way across the room.

My heart picks up its pace, a natural bodily response that now frustrates the living daylights out of me, knowing they can sense these sorts of shifts from within me. Deeply set fear rises delightfully through my body, warming my cheeks. Each pulse of blood through my veins is magnified, thrumming under my skin.

Axton's eyes darken, the usually bright emerald green shifting right before my eyes. His angular jaw flexes at the sides, flaring with each clench of his teeth. This time, it's as though I flicked a switch in him, not the other way around. I can see why he enjoys this feeling.

"Go on, Miah. Tell me she won't love the dark, depraved

world we call home. I know you can scent her just as well as I can." He stalks toward me, his eyes not leaving mine. I look up, feeling exposed. "Now, bring me some of the clothes you bought for her the other day, and let's delve into the darkness. Bring Cassius back too. He seems to have a soft spot for my human, and not in a way that makes me want to rip his throat out. An extra set of fire paws will be useful down there."

We are joined by Cassius, who is skulking behind us silently. His eyes flit from one dark corner to the next. My shoulders roll back, the crunch of my bones clicking together breaking the invisible tension lingering in the air. Both Cassius and Miah are strongly against us being here at all, the risk too high in their opinion. But my curiosity knows no bounds, and the debauchery of Hell lured me in, hook, line, and sinker.

My combat boots fall heavy on the black gravel, my short legs working hard to keep up with the pack. Axton is at least 6'7, with the two hellhounds being the size of a male grizzly bear; my short stature has absolutely no hope. Every few moments, Axton looks down at me, his eyes traveling up and down my entire body appreciatively. My cheeks warm at his forwardness, liking the look in his eyes when his focus is solely on me. *When the fuck did that happen?*

Part of me wants to slap the smirk off his face, but another revels in the rawness of his emotions. He isn't making a show of trying to hide it, not unless his father is around. He's perfectly readable at all times, and right now? Right now, he looks as though he wants to consume me entirely.

I'm wearing his button-up shirt, the side tucked into a black leather skirt that's so tight, it looks as though it's painted onto my skin. Around my waist is a belt, a snake's open mouth as the silver buckle. Thankfully, I was provided with my first pair of panties since coming here, although they are wedged tightly up my ass. Apparently, thongs are the only underwear he has to offer me.

The energy here is heavy and dark, the strong metallic scent of blood thick in the air, mixing with the smokey haze. It reeks of death and decay, a scent I am all too familiar with.

Shops line the streets, unkept and falling apart. Parts from the roofs spear through entryways, thick layers of dirt and grime covering every surface. It's almost like taking a step back in time, except there are giant demons with torn wings and broken horns here, small beings covered in black fur with curved horns and paws for feet.

Everywhere I look, there is more, overwhelming every sense I have. Screams sound off in the distance, blood curdling yelps of pain. This is what I had in mind when I thought of Hell, this exact picture, with a bit more fire and lava.

Anxiety starts to wind its way through my veins, sinking its teeth in the further down the street we walk. My heart picks up its already-rapid pace, eyeing the crimson-skinned demon who has her hands wrapped around a man's throat. She watches his life force drain with a fanged grin.

Kneeling to the lifeless corpse, she slices her barbed tail across his neck before collecting blood in the well of her palm. Bringing it up to her face, she drinks the crimson liquid, allowing some to drip down the sides of her mouth with a growl. It's a grotesque display, slurps and snarls proving she's enjoying her freshly caught prey.

"What is this place?" I whisper, barely audible, my breathing shallow. Cassius moves closer to me, his heated fur brushing over my clammy hands. He has barely spoken a word, other than to voice his disgust at Axton for bringing me here. But there is something about him that brings a sense of calm.

"This place is where the light never touches, where the

beasts roam and the demons are freer from the confines set by the seven. Where up there is very similar to your world, rankings and treaties. Order. Here it's the opposite. The devil's real playground." Axton grins, the red lights reflecting in his green eyes. He seems enamored by it, entranced. "I won't let a soul touch you, Wynn. You have my word. Enjoy the experience. Let your dark little soul out to play."

CHAPTER 12
BALE

It reeks of blood and stale piss down here, rivers of crimson flowing down the cracked gutters. My gums pulse where the fangs protrude, aching to sink through the flesh of my missing mate. Over a week has passed with nothing. Every shred of information we receive is that she is alive, and it's expected that the knowledge is enough. But to me, it fucking isn't.

The cravings are painful, my entire body forcing itself to exist as a shadow. Before, I managed without feeding much, sporadically sipping on demons or animals when the need arose. Now, a hunger unlike I have ever felt is forcing me down into the depths, where the demons break free of their confines.

A cesspit of deviance, and the only place in Hell where they sell fresh human blood on the black market. It won't fix things, I'm not that stupid. It may, however, curb the cravings enough to think rationally. This fucking haze will make me useless in the fight to get her back.

I pull my hood further down in an attempt to conceal my face, hoping no one recognizes me down here. Most of them likely know of the infamous vampire spawn of Satan. The scum will have heard of what goes on up above, but few will have laid eyes on me before, something I can use to my advantage.

A shrill scream sounds from somewhere in front of me, averting my eyes to a succubus slicing the throat of a male demon. What I feel in that moment stops me in my tracks, my fangs piercing my lower lip to stop the snarl threatening to escape. The pure need I have been feeling intensifies tenfold, physically moving my body of its own volition, as if my vampire side has taken over completely. As I fight my own willpower, the source of the overdrive comes into view.

Standing there is my little mate, her eyes entranced by the bloodbath in front of her. She's here, down in this dirty corner of Hell, a place she certainly shouldn't be, even with the security detail forming a V around her. Taking a deep breath, I dig my claws into my palms, the usual distraction of pain doing nothing to soothe the drive to get to her.

I step into the shadows, watching closely as her stunning blue eyes blow wide at the display. Her nose wrinkles to start with, but her disgust very quickly morphs into something else. Intrigue, maybe, as she leans forward, her once-sleek hair now knotted, draping over her shoulder.

My eyes are laser-focused on her, the rest of this place blurring and unimportant, like a beacon calling to every single part of me, body and soul. It takes everything in me to not run over there, pull out the hearts of the three beings surrounding her, and embalm them to give her as a gift. My girl would like that, with her deep fascination with the macabre. A little memento to remember the moment.

As if sensing I am here, she searches the shadows, looking right where I am but not seeing me. The darkness provides just the right amount of coverage. Her heart rate climbs, the thrum echoing through my ears. It's a symphony, music to calm the depths of my soul. The four of them continue down the winding path, and Wynn spins around to look at the darkness engulfing me several times along the way. She has to feel something, her hands clasping into fists and rubbing at her chest, as if she's trying to ease the pain.

They all come to a stop outside a broken down soulstone jeweler, the ding from the entry bell ringing to announce their arrival. Soulstones are illegal up above. The mining in the extreme lower depths is deemed too difficult for the princes to regulate, hence why the only place to get them is down in this shit hole. Demons here have little to live for, so taking the risk for the sake of a shiny black bit of stone is worth it when it sells as it does.

Hovering just outside the window, I watch the demon place a bit of material in the glass cabinet, opening each side slowly to reveal something that has Axton grinning ear to ear. Wynn stands in the middle of the group, unimpressed by whatever she has seen, arms crossed firmly across her chest. If he's trying to win her with something materialistic, he has another thing coming. The little demon show she witnessed earlier would mean more to her than a bit of jewelry.

A low growl rumbles from deep within my chest as I watch from the darkness. The way he touches my mark on her throat when securing the silver necklace around her delicate neck makes me want to rip his heart from his chest. Maybe she can have his fingers as well as his heart if they keep touching her like that. He hovers, whispering into her ear.

"This may sting, little human. Turn around and let me solder this in place."

"I'm assuming I don't get a choice in this?" she bites back with a snarl, her eyes pinned on him, nostrils flaring and jaw clenched. She's pissed. Good girl.

"You are walking around with his bite on your collarbone,

Wynn. If I am to take you out and parade you around as my father wishes, I need to at least stake some claim. Wearing my initials around your throat is a good start."

She laughs at Axton, taking a step closer to him, her finger pointed at his chest. Each nail is jagged and snapped, not the weapons they were at the academy. They are all perfectly sharpened to a point, enough to tear through clothes or skin.

"You have already made me wear nothing but your clothes for a week, asshole. If you are so bothered, give me a bloody turtleneck sweater. I am not a fucking dog who needs collaring."

He grabs her shoulders firmly, his fingers digging into her flesh through the shirt she's wearing. I am going to enjoy breaking them one by one, relishing in the snap of his bones, knowing he touched her. Within seconds, he has a green flame in his hand, holding the silver together. The scent of burnt hair floods my nostrils, skin and flesh singed. Waiting for the moment to strike is no longer an option with her in pain like this.

I throw myself through the door, every set of eyes in the room on me. Wynn attempts to run to me but is halted by Axton's hand gripping her neck from the back, making her yelp. The two hellhounds take that moment to whip around and stand in the space between us. A wall of mutt—great.

"I think you have something that doesn't fucking belong to you!" I snarl, closing the space further, coming face to face with both the beasts. The white one looks savage, rows of sharp teeth glistening in the faint light. The big, black one, on the other hand, is more concerned with my little mate, looking from her to me and back again.

"You came," Wynn breathes with a wince. He has burnt the skin on the back of her neck trying to fasten the collar, the scent lingering in my nostrils. My fangs ache to sink into her, to lick the crimson right from her skin. She's so close, so close

I can almost touch her, but there are a few hundred pounds of hellhound to cross first.

"Who's first?" I ask. My hand motions to each of the hounds before Axton, cracking my neck in preparation. It has been a few days since I felt the life drain from someone, but I'm about due. My eyes lock on the white hound, drool dripping from its mouth, wanting to rip me to shreds.

"Don't you dare touch a single bit of fur on her—or him, for that matter. So what, you kill these two who are the two beings other than myself that are trying to keep her safe, and then what? Try and kill me too?" Axton taunts, a sly grin on his face. He's a smug prick.

The demon in the store flees, leaving a trail of piss in his wake. For someone who lives and breathes down here in the depths, he has a weak stomach if this is too much for him. Pathetic thing deserves to be hidden in the lower levels, he would be eaten alive by those above him.

"It's cute you think I would need to try that hard to off your pompous ass, Axton. This shit, it's between your father and mine. It has nothing to do with my mate. Now, let her go."

Wynn's eyes blow wide, her breaths short and shallow. She's nervous and, from her scent, a little turned on. The sweetness mixed with sin on her is addictive, a scent I will never get sick of. She looks over to Axton, pleading with her eyes. "What use am I to you anyway? A prisoner to, what, follow around the house?"

His focus shifts to her, his hand gripping her chin and forcing her face closer to his. I try to step forward, snarling when I'm stopped by the two beasts in front of me. They stand closer to each other, minimizing the small gap between them.

"You have no idea just how important you are, do you? I have been trying to tell you since the day we met that I, like this asshole here, am one of your mates, but you refuse to see it. Masking your pull with attitude and snark. You're mine just as much as you are his."

He turns to look at me, a wide, shit-eating grin plastered across his face. This can't be happening. I shoulder through the two hellhounds, their teeth nipping at my limbs, trying to hold me back. Blood trickles down each slice, my clothes wet and clinging to me like a second skin. Wynn makes a move to push past him, but she is yanked back by her hair, the tattered lengths now twisted around Axton's fist. She snarls at him, her teeth bared. Fuck, I love the fire in her.

"Stop him, but don't kill him. They're bonded!" he yells, the sound muffled by the blood rushing to my ears. Claws come from both sides, a mash-up of teeth and paws slicing at every inch of skin. My hands swipe in an attempt to grasp any part of them I can get my hands on, sinking into nothing but air and smoke.

This isn't me, it isn't how I fight. The need to get closer to her holds my body prisoner, acting on pure instinct with only one thing at the forefront: getting to her. There's not an inch of self-preservation in sight.

Blood rushes from the wounds, pooling on the floor below me. My eyes don't leave hers as I push through the pain, ripping out chunks of fur and stabbing my claws into their flesh like daggers. But it isn't enough. My body is too weak from blood loss to physically reach her.

Dropping to the ground, I begin to crawl across the heated, wet ground on all fours, pushing past the intense pain until Wynn stands directly in front of me.

Sobs break through the whooshing in my ears, her pained cries burning into my mind forever. It's a sound I better fucking never hear again. I reach for her bare legs, my bloody hand marking her skin. She bends down, her hair dancing over my shoulder as she whispers into my ear.

"They will let you live if I go without argument. Heal. Heal, then come for me."

I snarl, my hands reaching out for her but catching on nothing. She's gone. *Again*. Only now, I am blessed with the knowledge this asshole might just be a bigger part of all this than we first thought.

CHAPTER 13
LUKA

The club is empty at this time of day, just barkeeps and the twins bustling around, preparing for the night ahead. The lack of movement on getting our girl back is grinding on all of us, but Bale has been fucking torturous. I love him; he's a part of me, the one person I have been able to rely on my entire life. But handling this side of him is tough when it takes everything I have to hold myself together, longing for the girl who is just out of reach, in the hands of people she shouldn't be.

So rather than being in his line of sight, I am sitting at the bar, drinking horrible creations to pass some time. Alexis pours me another drink, some bright green cocktail with silver glitter swirling through the liquid. She has been testing out some new drinks, using me as the guinea pig. May as well make use of me while I'm here.

"Alexander should be back in a minute. He was visiting Asmodeus today. Let's hope he has some news on your human." She grins, pushing the glass over the bar top in my direction. "In the meantime, try this. No questions, just drink."

It burns my mouth and throat, tasting like someone has poured fuel past my lips. The sting lingers, firing jolts of pain across my tongue. Luckily, we don't have to physically eat to satiate ourselves, because my taste buds are completely fried after that.

I inhale deeply; my nose has never been this clear in my life. My stomach heaves the moment the liquid hits, threatening to expel every last drop from my body. What in the world she put in this, I have no idea, but it's something I'm not in a rush to try again.

"Alexis, what in the fuck was that?"

Before she can answer, Alexander storms through the door, flinging it into the wall with a loud thud. He crosses the space in seconds, hopping over the bar and collecting his sister into his arms. Fangs clash and blood trickles down their faces with me as an unwilling witness.

"I missed you," she giggles, licking the trail of blood from his collar to his mouth, a low moan escaping. "I missed you too, sister."

Rising from the barstool, I start to walk out of the room when Alexander calls me back, his cool demeanor back in place. These two are absolutely addicted to one another, the need to consume each other in any way they can going above anything else.

"I spoke to Asmodeus. He said tomorrow, his VIP has been booked out by Lev and Axton, with arrangements for five. I assume he is going to start parading his little prize like we thought." He moves to take a sip of the green cocktail, spitting it out immediately. His lip pulls up in disgust until Alexis glares at him. "If I could offer some advice? Don't take your brother. He will be a slave to his instincts until he feeds off her again, making stupid decisions. Take your hellhound friend instead."

Excitement shoots through my veins, my chest feeling

lighter than it has since the night she was taken from us. This is the first whiff of information we have been able to gain, every other lead falling flat when we need it most. No one wants to take sides in what could be the first war in Hell, one we are more than willing to initiate if things don't start moving.

Tomorrow. Tomorrow, I get to lay eyes on the girl who stole parts of my very soul without even trying. The snarky little thing crawled into my veins and hooked her claws in. Alexander is right—Bale is not the being to take in this situation. One look at her would be all it took for him to tear through the room, leaving no survivors.

"We will come. Not with you two, but we will attend the club and keep our distance. Just in case."

It's quiet as I step through the front doors at home, save for the hushed whispers barely audible from my father's office. When we came back home to get our girl back, I assumed it would be the four of us working together, Bale, Pyro, father and myself kicking ass and taking names. Not necessarily happy about being together, but together, nonetheless.

Since being back, I expect Bale and Pyro to be closer after their little tussle in the pits, fostering a connection they absolutely need for her, if no one else. What I didn't expect, however, is hearing my father and Pyro having hushed conversations without me present. Bale's temper gets him excluded from a lot important meetings; the chaos isn't worth it when I can relay information after.

I hover just outside the door to the office, listening in on what the fuck this secret little meeting is about. My father and Pyro are in a heated conversation, the hellhound snarling at what Satan has to say. If Pyro has any self-preservation of any kind, he might want to rein in the feral side of himself. Although Wynn doesn't really know any of us that well yet, it will hurt her immensely if any of us die. Her heart would physically be in pain, or so I have heard.

My father spoke about the fates a little more depth the first night we arrived home, more about our mother too. He knows she is in pain, but he has no idea where she ran. The more I learn about these bonds and how they work, the more concerned I become for Wynn. She's feisty and full of fire, but she knows nothing about our world. She is stuck with none of us to guide her, to help her understand why her body craves ours, why her heart will start to ache or why there's a thrum of need that dances along her skin, pulling her toward all three of us, possibly four if what my father's little naked informant says is true.

"Just because he wasn't there doesn't mean she is in immediate danger, Pyro. Stand down until I know more, understand?" my father orders. His presence radiates through the walls. Who is he talking about?

"You can't go dangling a fucking carrot with her name on it in front of me to do your bidding. This contact is a bust, just like the rest. With all due respect, you need to step up to the plate and show what it means to fuck with one of your own," Pyro snarls in response, ballsy for someone who doesn't have a meaningful connection to my father outside of us. I wait, expecting anger to erupt, for my father to rip the throat out of the hound who has stood his ground, but it never comes. Silence falls over the room, the feeling heavy.

"Luka. Come in, son."

Shit.

Taking a deep breath, I walk into the office with every bit of confidence my body can muster. My wings sit proudly at my back, despite my resolve slipping. I need to keep my composure in place.

"Anyone care to tell me what's going on in here?" My brow raises as I stare directly at my father. Pyro is off to the side, his arms folded across his chest, jaw clenched. He's pissed, and I want to know why.

The air in here could be sliced with a blade, thick and raw. Neither are masking their emotions in any way, a demon's playground: anger, hatred, concern, all wrapped in a tight little capsule within the office.

"I have an informant in Lev's home," my father starts, moving to sit at his desk. "As soon as this all started, I planted him in there, just in case. I sent Pyro to see him. Both being hellhounds, I thought it would be less conspicuous, as we can't risk anyone finding out he is linked to us. Pyro went to meet him, and he was a no-show."

"You have had someone on the inside this whole fucking time and never thought to tell me?" I growl through clenched teeth. Rage simmers at the surface, needing an outlet before it explodes. "How long have you known?"

My glare pierces through Pyro as he stands straighter, eating the distance between us in two steps. He looks just as pissed as I am, but he should have told me, told *us*. We could have gone as more of a team instead of the three of us working on separate leads that have gotten us nowhere. But here we are, and to be honest, I am just as much at fault.

"Since last night. Don't go getting all shitty at me; blame him for giving a dodgy lead. Neither of you have been here to bounce any of this shit off, and I can't just sit here and wait for her to walk through the gates. I need to get to her, just like you two do."

"Look. We are getting next to nowhere working alone. I am just as much at fault here, I'm demon enough to admit that. But we need to actually work together. You know, as a team. Strength in numbers and all that bullshit." Looking between the two of them, they both nod slightly in response, neither saying a word. "I have a lead. It gets us closer to her to at least check she's alive and reasonably safe. Not on our land, so we can't kill all the fuckers with her and steal her back, but..."

"Give me a time and place. No more of this hidden bullshit either. From any of us." Pyro storms out of the room and slams the door behind him.

CHAPTER 14
AXTON

As soon as we arrived back yesterday, she pulled away, slamming the door to her room. I let her little dramatic moment unfold, huffing and puffing to pull the dresser into place to keep me out. Because it worked so well for her last time, not like I can't just climb through the window and slip in behind her again. No harm in indulging her.

The little human is testing me in her sleep. My molars grind to the point of fucking pain as she rolls her ass into my cock until she finds a comfortable spot. Her concept of danger concerns me, instincts should take over at some point. The flight response when you are in the face of danger is natural, but she grinds her ass up against it or slams doors in its face.

She has received more kindness from me than any other being, but that doesn't change what I am to my very core: a demon, one who has been resisting nature since this human walked into the Keep. If I give in, everything changes.

My fingers trace the mark left by her angry little vampire, who is likely limping back home with his proverbial tail between his legs by now. He will heal; it might just take a little while. Goosebumps spread across her exposed skin, a slight shiver shooting down her spine. I toy with the little A dangling from the dainty metal collar I had made for her, the one soldered with hellfire around her throat yesterday before Bale rudely interrupted us.

A light knock sounds at her door, the dresser screeching across the floor moments later. She barely moves, shifting her body around so it's facing mine and snuggling back into my chest. My father appears at the doorway with a stern look on his face. This isn't going to be fun.

I slowly slide out of bed, pulling the blankets up to her shoulders and sliding a pillow where I was so she doesn't wake up. The best part of my mornings is surprising her and waiting for her body to react to mine.

"Come. Tonight, we are taking her out, and there are some ground rules you need to be aware of." We step into his office, no pleasantries required with no one around to impress, no one to scare.

"What do you need from me, father?" I ask, flopping down onto one of the chairs in the corner of the room. There are pieces worth small fortunes scattered through the office, one being a saber-tooth tiger's tooth sitting on a small black stand. He hates anyone touching his precious things, a bit of a sore point. Picking up the tooth, I place the pointed end on the tip of my finger, twirling it until small rivulets of blood flow from the impact point. Good luck getting the stain out, asshole.

"I need you to pull your finger out of your ass and accept my gift in its entirety. You need to bond with the girl before tonight, when we take her on her first public outing. She needs to reek of you." My father's nostrils flare as he watches me toy with his priceless antique. "All you had to do was fuck the human. She doesn't need to be wooed."

"Well, you should have been a little more specific with

your instructions. You asked for me to keep her in line and gain her trust, both of which I have excelled at, wouldn't you say?" I spin the tooth again, not even bothering to look up.

He doesn't understand the implications of it, bonding with the girl. My body aches for her, needing to have a taste, but alongside her comes another three beings, all of whom will stop at nothing to get her back. There is no way to get through to him when his tunnel vision is like this, though, so I will have to deal with the other three assholes at a later date, it seems.

His fist slams down on the heavy wooden desk, rattling the rare trinkets adorning the top. The only thing in this room he will risk breaking is me, but he needs me all pretty to show off tonight, so I'm reasonably safe.

"It was me who took the girl, and I can just as easily discard her. If you fail, Silas and I will fuck her in your place, and you know how that ends for the demons. Just imagine what we would do with a breakable little human. Silas has killed a woman with that hellhound dick of his, piercing it through her insides until she vomited blood."

Rising from the chair, I close the space between us before throwing the sharpened, blood-stained fang at him with unmatched precision. It embeds itself into his shoulder; it's not far enough to do damage unfortunately, but it will scar.

He calls out my name with enough venom to terrify anyone around us, but I don't look back, not with a threat like that hanging over her head. There is not a doubt in my mind at this point that the defiant human is my mate. No fucking way am I letting my father anywhere near her, or his ruthless little pet.

The shower is running by the time I get back, steam billowing from behind the cracked door. This will have been the first morning she has woken up alone since being forced down here. It will also mark the day she is properly mated to me, regardless of her resistance. It's me or him, a choice between life or death in every sense of the word.

A rich jasmine scent floods my senses, mixing with the steam in the room. Standing in the doorway, I spend time taking her in without the constant stream of curse words and fire. The way the water glides over her curves has me salivating, itching to get my hands on her, to mark her skin, to taste her. I ache to chase her through a forest of black and gray, only to brighten it with flashes of red. All the restraint I built was crushed by his orders, opening the floodgates to the obsession lingering under the surface.

She gets out, wrapping herself in one of the lush towels, looking up at me through her wet lashes. "Do I not get a shred of fucking privacy in this place? Want to watch me pee too?"

A laugh rumbles through my chest as I approach her, grasping her chin firmly and forcing it up. Her stable heartbeat starts to rise, becoming more rapid each moment we stand here. She is drawn to me, just as I am to her. She just doesn't quite understand it yet.

"If piss play is something you're into, just say so. I wouldn't say no to any form of depravity you put forward." I smile, watching her expression twist into disgust. What she doesn't realize is, not a word of it is a lie. It wouldn't be the top item on my list, but I would without question.

"Listen closely, little human. I've been as patient as my nature allows. Get dry and put some clothes on, preferably with those heavy-duty boots Miah bought for you," I order, a slight smirk tipping the corner of my lips. She looks pissed, nostrils flared and jaw tight, like she's moments away from slapping me. This could be interesting.

"Fuck off, Axton. Don't think I have forgotten what you did yesterday, beating the ever-loving Christ out of Bale, and for what? You're a piece of shit!" she spits, her voice laced with venom. If she thinks this will make me leave her alone, she has another thing coming. My dick twitches, pressing harder against the seam of my boxers, reacting to the fire she throws my way.

I cage her in, one arm on either side of her, white-knuckling the stone bench she backed herself into. Her slick body trembles, the water running down her chest a distraction. My eyes follow the drops, and I itch to lean down and lick them off her skin.

"He's fine, Wynn. You would feel it if he wasn't. That precious beating organ in your chest is racing, but not from the pain of losing a bonded mate. For the record, I didn't lay a single finger on the fanged asshole. I even told them not to kill him. What more did you want?"

"For you to let me go, Axton. It isn't rocket science. I'm a prisoner here, held against my will!" she snaps, tears welling in her bright blue eyes. She doesn't fucking understand the consequences of letting her go, what that means for not only her, but all of us. Her emotions are raw, frustration being the most prominent.

"Let me make myself clear. If I let you go yesterday, none of us would have woken up today. You would have been thrown into a cell with whatever was most hungry in his creature zoo. Miah and Cassius would have been turned into smoking piles of ash." I lean in, my face inches from hers. "And me? The darkness rotting my heart would have taken over completely, rendering me dead inside. This may be a fucking surprise, but I didn't want to hurt your precious mate. I had to."

"I..." She goes to speak, cut off by my lips crashing to hers. Hesitating for a moment, she opens her lips only a touch, allowing me to fucking devour her. My hands drop to her ass, picking her up before placing her on the counter without breaking our kiss. Her legs spread enough for me to pull her close, my cock straining against her heat.

Not that she would believe me if I tried to tell her, but this is a first for me. I'm not one to romance something that merely fills a need to rid myself of pain, so kissing has never appealed to me. But with her, the taste is even sweeter than I thought. Her teeth clamp down hard on my lower lip, the blunt edges unable to break the skin.

"I know you're pissed. I get it. But don't keep fucking denying this pull between us. I know you feel it, or you sure as shit wouldn't have this reaction to me. I'm no incubus." I grind myself harder against her pussy, watching her scowl soften, her hips pushing harder against mine. "Let me make it up to you. Let me show you just how much I want to worship you."

"You think I'm the type who wants to be worshiped, huh?" she jokes, a hint of challenge in her tone. "I don't forgive you for what you had them do to him."

"Never said you had to forgive me, Wynn. I don't have the power to go back in time and change it, and even if I did, it would have likely turned out the same. What I asked is for you to break down that barrier and let go, even if just for tonight."

Her heart races as she stares up at me silently, torn between fighting or giving in, wrangling her thoughts. I could shift her emotions, flick on the lust, and leave it at that. Before I even have the time to ponder it, she nods, her hands splaying across my chest and pushing me from between her thighs.

"If you ever lay a single fucking finger on them again, I will make it my personal mission to ensure darkness consumes your broken heart. Do you understand?"

I fight the smirk threatening to emerge, my teeth biting into my tender lower lip. There is no doubt in my mind she has the potential to make good on her deal, tearing the small amount of soul in my body to little pieces. The woman would probably try to keep it as a trophy from what Miah has told me about their conversations.

"I understand. Now, as I was saying, get dressed and get your ass downstairs to the back entrance of the Keep. You have five minutes before I come back and drag you down by your hair." A feather-light whimper slips from her lips, enjoying the idea of that a little too much.

CHAPTER 15
AXTON

Her excitement reaches me before she even opens the door, her wide eyes scanning the grounds to find me. She walks out in a pair of combat boots, fishnet stockings under her black and white plaid skirt. My shirt hangs low on her short frame, hitting just above the hem. She's a vision in black.

"Well, what now?" she calls with a grin, taking in the landscape around her. The burnt trees and swirling smoke are not as picturesque as she's used to, but they're fitting for the dark little soul she seems to be. The longer I wait, the faster her heart races in anticipation, the rapid thump echoing through my ears. She has resisted up until now, feigning anger in place of heat, biting back rather than giving in to what her body craves.

Shifting from my place on the small gabled roof above the door she walked out of, I hop down behind her. My hands circle around that delicate throat, her pulse slamming into my fingertips, each gulp of air traveling past my grip. One small squeeze would be all it took, her life force so fragile in the hands of a demon. Leaning in until my lips are level with her ear, I run my forked tongue along the side of her neck, a little taste before the fear truly kicks in.

"Run."

As soon as my hands unfurl from her throat, she is off darting to the tree line, her skirt blowing above her ass in the wind. It takes everything I have to give her a head start. My instincts push me to fucking chase, but if I take off now, she will be stripped bare before she hits the trees.

She weaves in and out of the blackened tree trunks, the sticks snapping underfoot with each step. Mentally counting down from ten, I wait. My eyes focus on her body getting further and further away, her scent still lingering as if she never left, and fuck, if it doesn't turn me on. My cock thickens, painfully pressing against my zipper; this is not exactly the ideal outfit choice for a run.

Three.

Two.

One.

I lunge, a grin spreading across my face. Smoke swirls from my feet, my wings tucked firmly at my back. If I flew, it would be too quick, giving less time for the fear to sink its teeth in. I want my pretty little human terrified, turned on *and* terrified. Her breaths are short and rapid, skin dripping in sweat.

She turns around up ahead, her eyes darting from one tree to the next, her chest heaving. Bright blue eyes settle on my approaching figure, her teeth biting into her plump lower lip with a grin.

"Giving up already, Wynn? I expected more," I taunt, still approaching her at speed. Her brow raises as she sticks her middle finger up, darting off further into the dense woodland. "Let's see how brave you are with my hands wrapped around your throat."

Shaking my head, I follow, upping my pace. Stray branches slice at my skin, blood seeping from the thin webbing on my wings. The lick of pain pushes me harder, more demon than man at this point. Lust pours from her in waves, heady and intoxicating, my hunger intensifying the closer I get.

I reach out, wrapping her long, black hair around one of my fists. I yank back with every bit of power I have, dropping her body forcefully to the ground. Her breathing hitches, panic spreading across her stunning features. Those blue doe eyes widen as she struggles to suck in enough air to fill her lungs. I focus on her emotions, willing them to settle, easing the panic just enough for her breathing to catch back up before I lean down to her level.

"Playtime is over, little human. Now, it's time to feast."

She thrashes in my hold, her limbs flying out aimlessly but connecting with nothing. There's no hint of anger, nothing sinister. There's just pure lust and fear, swirling inside her to become one. She's like a drug, feeding my demon side in a way nothing else ever has. My very first addiction.

"You have been a defiant little thing," I snarl, licking the stray tears falling down the sides of her face, reveling in the salty taste, "denying that pull you feel. The pure fucking need runs through your veins just as heavy as it does mine."

She rolls her tongue around her cheeks, not expecting my mouth to open the second her lips part to spit at me. It lands on my tongue, spurring the need that little bit more. The drive to taste her takes over any rational part of me that wants to take this slow, to savor the moment.

Her eyes are pinned to my mouth, watching intently as I swallow everything she just gave, a whimper escaping her lips. She shakes her head, snapping out of whatever trance the moment had put her in.

"You think a little spit is going to scare me off?" I laugh, low and gravelly. I watch her writhe beneath my hold, her body at war with itself. If only she would give in and relish in the connection between us.

"I..." she trails off, looking anywhere but directly at me, her voice laced with need. "I don't understand what is happening to me."

"What's happening is that you are drawn to your mates. Your body craves them." My tongue dances across her bite mark from Bale, creating goosebumps across her pale skin. "And that includes me."

With that, I bite over his mark, hard enough to draw blood. The taste of her essence blooms on my tongue, my eyes rolling back. Fuck. I'm a demon, there is no doubt about that, but that first drop of her blood to hit my tongue forces a need from me I don't expect.

Wynn yelps, her head moving to the side for better access, a whispered moan escaping her lips. Her arousal intensifies, the scent flooding all my senses. Sweetness and sin, blood and lust. Curiosity laces my mind, knowing she fucked at least one of the others. The perfectly placed indents from Bale's teeth now jar with my own.

"Tell me, did you fuck them all already?" I ask, running my nose along the column of her throat, breathing in as much of her as my body allows. "Did they give your body what it needs?"

She snarls, thrashing aimlessly under me, knowing it will do nothing but grind her warm pussy against me. The fire in her turns me on to no end, my cock straining painfully against the heat of her core.

One of my hands travels down, flicking her skirt up and her panties to the side. They are drenched, her arousal seeping through the thin material. I glide my fingers across her clit lightly, her hips bucking up to chase my touch. She won't admit it, but she's a needy little thing.

"This. I need to fucking taste this." I cup her pussy firmly before slapping it, the echo bouncing off the bare trees. "Your fight turns me on, little human, but don't push it too far. This body is too fragile and breakable, and my restraint is already at its limit."

She looks me dead in the eyes, her breathing steady. I allow her to touch me, her hands delicately running over my arms before she wraps both firmly around my throat and squeezes. It's cute she's trying, but her strength is no match for my body.

Her hands pull until we are nose to nose, her body twitching under mine. Three words are all it takes for me to explode. Three simple words pass her lips, and my restraint disappears into thin air, as if it never existed to begin with. The beating heart in her chest escalates at her declaration, excitement and need thrumming through her veins.

"Then break me."

Within seconds, I have her body flipped, her knees digging into the sticks and dirt beneath us. My hands pull at the fabric still covering her body, ripping and tearing until she is left in nothing but her combat boots. The fishnets are torn and laying on the ground with the rest of the fabric shreds.

I push her chest toward the ground, her pussy now exposed completely. It's not like I haven't seen her naked before, but seeing her like this, all raw and exposed...she's complete and utter perfection.

My fingers dig into the flesh of her upper thighs, giving me better access to her. I drag my forked tongue from her clit to her ass, my eyes rolling back at the taste of her arousal. She pushes herself back, leaning into my touch, a low growl aimed at me.

"You taste fucking delectable," I breathe against her pussy, her body shaking in my hold. My tongue swipes at her clit, increasing the pressure until I feel her limbs tense. She's close, a mix of spit and her arousal dripping from my chin as I devour her completely.

My fingers grip her trembling muscles tighter, enough that

she will have pretty purple bruises in the shape of me wrapped around each thigh. Marked. Mine. The thought alone has me moaning, the vibration through my tongue being the last straw.

She screams out, loud enough for the dread ravens to fly into the sky. Her thighs clamp together, aftershocks zapping through her as my tongue glides inside her, not wanting to waste a drop. The need to be inside her, to fuck her into oblivion, turns me wild. My demon side is well and truly in control, driven to bond with her in the most primal way possible: cock deep inside her to the hilt, siphoning every emotion she exudes to feed the addiction while that slight knot forces its way past any resistance.

Tearing my clothes from my body, I position myself behind her, admiring her glistening pussy. She turns her head to the side, lust-filled eyes hazed over by tears. Her teeth bite into her plump lower lip hard as she takes in the sight behind her.

I'm completely naked, my large black wings extended on either side, tail snaking around my body to touch her. The razor edge lightly drags up the back of her thigh, leaving a light red mark in its path before swapping to the other side. She hasn't seen me like this yet, complete demon, tail and all. The near-useless appendage has been more of an annoyance until this moment, teasing her skin.

"Please," she pleads, an unexpected word falling from her now-bloodied lip. Pleading isn't something I ever expected to tumble out of her mouth, but she has me curious.

"Please what, Wynn? Use your words."

"Make it hurt," she grits out, her fingers digging into the dirt. "I...I need you to make it hurt."

Swirling my tongue over my cheeks, I spit onto my hand, gliding it over the head of my cock before lining up with her entrance. My grip on her hips has to be painful, my restraint crumbling completely, that thin thread tethering my control gone.

"Remember what you begged for," I breathe through clenched teeth, my cock against her pussy. One of my hands reaches for her neck, pushing her face further into the dirt. My cock eases into her inch by inch until I reach the very edge. Waiting a moment for her to adjust, I tighten my grip before unleashing.

My pace is feral, but she meets every single thrust, slamming her ass against me. I let my tail rake down her spine, splitting the skin only just. Blood starts to pool in the valley between her ribcage, running down her sides.

"Is this what you wanted?" I snarl, her pussy gripping my cock in a vice-like hold. It takes all of me to not explode there and then, to fill her full of my cum, marking her for anyone who comes into contact with my little mate.

I pull out of her, flipping her body over and slamming her down. My cock slides back inside her while my hands wrap around her throat. She's a mess of dirt and blood, tears streaming down her temples. Nothing but pure lust pours from her, the emotion overpowering everything else. Taking this moment, I look down at the display, siphoning everything she has to offer.

The moment has my head spinning, drunk on her. I'm unsure if humans feel the euphoria of a bond snapping into place, the overwhelming need to possess and protect. My body needs to be closer to hers despite being as deep inside her as I can get. The swell at the base of my cock enters her like her pussy is made to fit me.

Her eyes roll back, curses falling out of her mouth between each ragged breath. A guttural moan tears through me as her pussy clamps down, her body writhing under my hold, taking everything I have to give. I can feel her pulse racing through my fingertips, her little heart trying and failing to keep up.

My grip on her tightens, her breath struggling to pass under my brutality. Her eyes widen as I bury myself as deep as my cock can go, my release flooding her pussy. She thrashes, her hands firmly holding mine around her throat while she explodes around me. Her all dirtied, marked and bitten, fighting under me as she comes is a fucking vision.

It takes a few minutes for the swelling to go down, enough for me to ease out of her without pulling her hips with me. She whines under me, completely and utterly spent, not wanting to move a muscle. My fingers trace each side of her entrance, forcing her to shiver under my touch.

"Did I hurt you like you wanted, little human?" I push my release back into her pussy, and it pulses around my fingers despite how tender she has to be. I wasn't gentle on her, the force brutal and hard against her soft flesh.

She smirks back at me, the answer on the tip of her tongue as she contemplates whether now is the time to push my buttons. What she doesn't know is that in this moment, she could get away with just about anything.

"The big, bad demon isn't as scary as he thinks."

CHAPTER 16
WYNN

My entire body is overwhelmed, tremors moving through each muscle fiber, forcing my body to twitch in Axton's arms. He has been silent the entire walk back to the Keep, his jaw tense, flaring at the sides with his eyes focused solely on me. The clothes I came here in lay in a pile amongst the trees, rendered useless from his brutality.

He passes the room I have been staying in since being here, up another flight of stairs to the very top. Eight beeps sound before the door clicks, swinging open to a space I haven't seen yet. There isn't much time to take it all in, his steps long and sure, passing through the rooms with no hesitation. A demon on a mission.

I'm lowered onto the softest bedding my skin has touched, the fibers a welcome change from the dirt and sticks of the forest floor. My skin feels tacky with a mix of sweat, blood, and dirt. I can only imagine the state I'm in, and yet he placed me down with a level of care I didn't expect.

My mind is at war with itself. Guilt swirls through my gut, forcing the bile to start bubbling deep in my throat. The feeling is unexplainable, like I am being pulled in multiple different directions, utterly confused and yet sure at the same time. There is a tangible pull with Axton, my body aching to be closer to him even though he is an entitled prick most of the time.

Yet that pull is present with Bale, Luka, and Pyro as well, an innate need that goes beyond rational thought, one I can't make sense of. They talk of the fates, all these beings down here, how lives are set to cross paths and all the nonsense that goes along with it. It happens in the spicy books I read all the time.

But for someone like me, who has been alone for the best part of their existence, this doesn't feel right. Having anyone with a need to be around me, speaking to me in the way they do, is foreign to me. Being looked at with pure need the way they do. The feeling of actually wanting to be around anyone, when I have preferred solitude for as long as I can remember, so this is novel.

The sound of the shower running pulls me from my thoughts, and I pray the shower is for me. Lord knows I need it. My body tenses as I shift on the bed, the pain pulsing through my lower stomach. He went easy on me, something I am well aware of, holding himself back. It intrigues me to know what it would be like if he didn't.

He walks back in, a dark green towel wrapped low around his waist. For the first time, his wings are not out, just the same black horns jutting through the mess of dark hair. The man looks like a god wrapped in the body of a demon. He reaches down, emerald eyes staring into mine with an air of uneasiness, like he is scared to touch me.

Without even thinking, my hand connects hard with his cheek—admittedly not the best reaction to have when the man could change his mind and kill me in an instant. The slap sends pins and needles through my hand, leaving a red mark with specks of dirt and dried blood across his chiseled cheek.

"What the fuck was that for?" he snarls, his face now inches from mine.

"You chase me through the woods, fuck me in the dirt, then carry me back here. The last is done while giving me the silent treatment and looking at me like I am about to break into a thousand pieces." My body shifts to the edge of the bed, forcing him to take a step back while I stand, a little wobbly on my feet.

Reluctantly, he moves back as I shoulder past him, making a b-line for the still-running shower. He closes in behind me, his hand gripping the back of my neck and swinging me like a rag doll to face him. Anger radiates from him, heaving breaths and all, anger he focuses on me. I probably shouldn't have slapped him. It did feel really good, though.

"Because you have every chance of breaking into a thousand little pieces, little human. Then what?" he growls as his grip tightens on my neck, forcing a whimper from my throat. "We are bonded. That concept is foreign to you, but it sure as shit isn't to me. If your body breaks, if you break, I break. The difference is, your death is quick. I am immortal. My pain will last the rest of what will be a fucking miserable existence."

"I'm sure another pretty little human will cross paths wi..." I start, but he slaps his hand across my mouth.

"No. You don't get to be smart with me about this, Wynn. I crave that fire in you, but you are not going to belittle this. I hate those fucks you are fated to, but they face the same fate—though mostly the black-haired fanged asshole because of this." He places his hand over the bite mark on my collarbone. "But all of them have something to lose if you die."

Unwanted tears well in the corners of my eyes, my lashes clumping with the water and dirt. I'm not a crier; emotion is a fickle thing that never really made much sense to me. Pain, fear —they are tangible, a reaction to something.

He releases his hand from my mouth, staring at me with sincerity as he wipes the stray tear from my cheek then licks it from the pad of his thumb. "Now, unless my cock is balls deep inside that heavenly cunt of yours, slapping me isn't a very good idea. Come; as much as the sight of you all dirty makes me hard, we have somewhere to be in a few hours. Your first royal outing."

I am dragged to the bathroom and plunged under the huge rain showerhead, the temperature searing, just how I like it. My hand wraps around his wrist, pulling him under as well. The harsh lines of his body look even better covered in water. Swirls of crimson travel down his abdominal muscles, part of me wanting to run my tongue along the ridges. He starts to lather up a loofah with a soap that smells completely of him.

"I can see your brain ticking over. Just let me touch you. Fight me about it tomorrow." His brow raises, waiting for a reaction that never comes. Large hands consume my small frame, scrubbing at every inch until my skin is pink and raw. "I prefer you all dirty and bloody, to be honest, but tonight, you are to be a little show pony."

"Excuse me?" I respond, my hands splayed out just below his pecs, pushing him away. "Please repeat the last part, because I'm sure you just referred to me as a fucking horse."

He huffs a solemn laugh, one void of any genuine joy. Grabbing my waist, he picks me up and sandwiches me between his torso and the black marble shower wall. Water pelts down onto both of us, filling the silence as my legs instinctively wrap around his waist to stop myself from sliding. The move has him growling, just as he had earlier tonight.

One hand grips my ass, the other wrapping around my throat, his thumb tilting my chin up to look at him. Why is it so fucking hot when he does that? He forces me to stare into his eyes, the emerald orbs seeing straight into my dark little soul.

His forked tongue makes another appearance. It snakes out and tastes a trail from the bite mark to my ear, nipping on it lightly. My pussy hurts from his intrusion, but that gesture has it tightening, asking for more of whatever he has to give.

"I kept you hidden for as long as I could, but he has plans. You were not stolen just to see if you were fated to me; you're a pawn just like I am, a piece in his chess set, and he's ready to play his hand with you."

"Can you help me get off the chess board, Axton? Both of us?" I ask, knowing the answer. Miah has let it slip Lev wouldn't hesitate to throw me down in the cells just as he threatened and that Axton's treatment would be worse. His lip twitches, almost like he knows what I'm thinking. Small scars litter his skin, flecks of pink and silver, the most noticeable being his lip. Part of me wants to lick it, to trace my tongue over the scars.

"We would be dead as soon as the breath fills our lungs as two people free from his wrath. Me being his son offers us no protection in the slightest." He runs his nose along my throat, inhaling deeply, a low rumble coming from his chest. "If he had to choose between ridding the underworld of his only son to ever exist or having that same son go against his orders, you bet your sweet ass he would pick the former."

He carries me over to the tiled bench in the shower, sitting me down and spreading my thighs until the muscles burn. My body is on complete display yet again, the demon looking at me like he wants to consume me whole, only to spit me out and fuck me. Sharp canines pierce through the skin on my inner thigh as he clamps his teeth down on the flesh. I whimper, my body warming, knowing it probably physically can't take him again but wanting it anyway.

"I won't fuck you again, not until we are back from the club at the very least. I can't even lick this pretty cunt clean, either, because I need you to be leaking down your thighs as we walk in. Every fucking demon in that place will know you're mine."

"Or, you could, I don't know...fuck me again?" I challenge, my hands tracing lightly over his small black horns. It would hurt, but there's no denying the need lingering heavier now than it did before the forest. It's like it intensified everything I felt previously, the pull. My body is hypersensitive to his touch. His tongue drags along the bite mark on my thigh, catching the trail of blood before shifting his eyes back to mine.

"Tempting, but we are already running late, and I am going to need more than a few minutes to get my fill of you. Miah will be here in a minute with some makeup, and the gown is hanging in my closet. You will stay in here from now on."

He reaches down between my thighs, his fingers gathering the small amount of our release to push it back inside me before putting them in his mouth. "Not a single fucking drop of you will be wasted ever again. Now, let's give these assholes a show."

It has all happened so quickly, being thrown into this world of creatures I didn't know existed, being told I am a part of it all in some fucked up way. But I know I feel the same pull to Pyro, Luka, and Bale that I do with Axton, the innate need to be around them, to be close to them. My body reacts to theirs in ways it hasn't around anyone before. The more time spent around any of them, the more this story becomes believable. The thought excites the hell out of me as much as it terrifies me.

CHAPTER 17
BALE

Consciousness slips in and out of the black void of my mind, voices whispering, loud thuds breaking through the deafening silence. My body is being dragged along the ground by a set of razor-sharp teeth, rocks digging into my flesh with each step. I attempt to fight, willing the feeling to filter through to my limbs, but nothing happens. The dull spark of life drops off faster than I can fuel it.

Suddenly, the motion stops, and I'm thrown onto what could be the ground. Hard and unforgiving, it sears heat through my cool skin. I wouldn't be surprised if a part of me is left behind when I regain enough strength to move.

"He's alive, sir. Barely, but alive," a low, deep voice says from beside me as heavy pressure forms on my sternum. "I could kill him; he is on our grounds now, one less of the bastards to deal with. They are not a risk now, but this here is the fucked up one. It's pure luck he is already half bled out, to be honest. Not sure if I could take him otherwise."

"These fucking vamps are all the same, stupid creatures who act on instinct alone. No better than your kind, slaves to nature."

Tingles move from my fingertips, slowly inching their way across my skin. Awareness seeps through my pores and sparks me back to life as my body starts to heal, knitting itself together piece by piece, fiber by fiber, fusing my flesh until blood is able to flow freely without constriction.

My eyes flit open, lashes clumped together with dried blood, the space blurred by unshed tears. There looks to be only the two figures here, standing in the dark with my near-lifeless body.

I just wanted to get to her, to be close to her. My body is running on instinct, just as the voice said. When instinct kicks in, there is usually bloodshed, bordering on a massacre —body parts strewn everywhere, severed from their vessel with me at the center, but this time, there was hesitation. I didn't trust myself not to hurt her in the fit of rage that overcame me, the need for her warring with the drive for blood.

"Ahh, there he is, the reject son." One of the figures kneels, his face closer to mine. My fangs snap in his direction, likely not anywhere near him. "What a gift you are. Now, what to do? Do I put you down in the cells to starve just like her, or do I kill you?"

His tail cuts a line down my cheek, the skin splitting painfully as my body tries to heal from the inside out. My arms reach to swipe at him but are stopped mid-air and pushed to the ground. Each blink clears my eyes just enough that the figure becomes clearer: a demon, one I now recognize. Lev.

Using the small amount of energy left in my body, I thrash under the pressure, my arms coming free. I can't feel or scent her in any way—there's no risk to her if I lose every shred of control I have left, which was minimal to start.

My claws slice through flesh, the feeling of fresh blood trickling through the webs between my fingers spurring me on more. The heavy weight lifts from my chest, a groan of pain echoing across the edges of my consciousness, one that doesn't come from me.

Diving forward, I sink my fangs into Lev's throat. I tear a jagged piece of flesh from his skin, spitting it out beside me. He may taste like shit, but his blood is ancient. It's potent enough to force the invisible threads weaving through my body to work faster, my strength flowing back rapidly. I'm going to need it if I want to get past these two. Both of them now in front of me poised for a fight I'm more than willing to provide.

"You wanna play, then stop fucking hesitating!" I snarl, his blood leaking down my chin, mixing with my own. The hellhound at his side stalks around me, the heavy smoke catching in my lungs, but neither of them make their move. Just as I go to spin, taking out the hellhound at my back, Lev's hand wraps around my throat, lifting my thrashing body into the air.

"You will soon learn your lesson, one that father of yours should have taught you long ago. I'm not one to be fucked with," Lev snaps right in my face. The heat from his hand is near unbearable. My limbs kick out as the darkness starts to take over, the pure rage fueling my every move. My fists fill with fur, blood pouring over my hands, but it's not enough.

The room blurs, oxygen denial starting to tug me in and out of consciousness for short amounts of time. Small words cut through the fog, broken in nature but enough to give one last push with every single shred of energy I have left.

Satan.
Kill.
Wynn.
Selene.

Fury rips through me, my teeth bared and snapping at anything within my radius. My claws drag up the arms of the demon holding me by the throat, cutting deep gauges through the muscles, but he doesn't let go. He grips me tighter, shaking me while sharp teeth tear at my limbs.

My head spins as small stars form behind my eyelids every time I blink, and the world tilts on its axis. Emerald green eyes bore into mine, laced with the pure evil they are attached to. His laughs begin to fade as the darkness takes over, flowing over me like waves to a shore. They edge closer with each round, taking more of my awareness until everything goes black.

CHAPTER 18
PYRO

The energy in the room is heavy, with concern and anger colliding to create a heady mix of emotions. No one has seen or spoken with Bale since I siphoned his emotions from the next room. I'm the last one of us to know he was here. At first, no one seemed concerned. Apparently, it's something he does quite often, fucking off without a trace. The story adds up there.

"He's my twin. I know it's hard for you to understand some things when it comes to the two of us, but I can feel it. Something isn't right." Luka paces, his wings scraping along the wood floor with each step. "This is more than him going off on his own. He's hurt or something. Not dead, but hurt."

"I will go out personally and look for him, Luka. You and Pyro have a job to do tonight. Go check that your mate is okay, and I will deal with this." Satan rakes his hands through his tousled platinum hair, looking more unkept than the last time I saw him. Dark rings are prominent under his tired eyes. "You have my word. Now, go, and don't do anything stupid. Tonight isn't about stealing her back in front of them; it's about making sure she is okay. Make them look less in front of anyone, and they will not hesitate to kill her."

Luka stops in his tracks, his brows shooting up as his eyes bore into his father's intensely. Looking at the two of them is like looking at the exact same person, one slightly bigger and older, their features and mannerisms are nearly identical.

"He's right. I know you don't know Lev or Axton all that well, but he will slit her throat and devour her flesh in front of us if there is any sign of showing him up. The demon is fucking ruthless," I respond, my arms cross over my chest. Luka has some control, I know that, but he is also young and impulsive. Less so than his twin, but he needs to know what he is up against.

"He will toy with you to lure a reaction out. He's addicted to provoking emotions, using things he has that they don't. In this case, your mate. Just, think before you react," Satan orders, downing the rest of his whiskey. "And should that fail, you are to hold my son back. Let those elusive shadows out to play and restrain him before you all get hurt or killed."

Asmodeus' club glows across the darkness of Hell, pink seeping through the smoke, visible for miles. Bass thrums beneath us, pulsing through the soles of my feet as we approach the door. Luka nods at the demon at the door, instantly gifting us with quick entry. Stepping over the threshold forces us through a wall of lust, emotions running so thick, you can almost see the fucking particles. It's potent enough to feel it on your skin like a sheen of sweat, sticking to the fine hairs.

Within seconds, we both feel her, looking in the same direction through the crowd. Luka goes to run, his body lurching forward just in time for my hand to grip his wing and yank him back. I feel the electricity, the pull, the near palpable string luring me in to get to her. But rash decisions are exactly what Lev wants.

Two ethereal vampires walk toward us, their eyes pinned to the grip I still have on Luka's wing. A familiar smile spreads across the woman's face, her eyes softening on approach. These two must be Luka's contacts, the ones who told him she would be here. The man nods at me, his jet-black hair falling into his face, and the woman spins Luka and pulls him into a tight embrace.

"So much for keeping your distance and staying lowkey, Alexis," Luka whispers, audible only to the four of us in close vicinity. "You really showed them you have nothing to do with me."

My focus shifts to the ledge above the main stage where my little mate is. As sweet as this little reunion is, I need to see her. She is in one of the VIP lounges, one with a full view of the large stage in the middle. At the moment, two demons hang out of a suspended cage above it.

Their lower halves are exposed and bent at the waist, both being fucked wildly by hellhounds in their true form. Grunts, moans, and screams fill the club, mixing with the loud music. In the middle of the cage sits a succubus, all four of her limbs tied to the bars, leaving her open to both the demons with their top halves trapped. What they are doing in there is hidden by the male demon's body, but from the screams, she is having a damn good time. The view is erotic as fuck, but nothing compares to Wynn. My cock doesn't even twitch at the display—not that I need more proof I'm hers, but if I did, this proves it.

My eyes stay trained on the balcony up there, hoping for a glimpse, anything, an indication she is reasonably okay. That her body is in one piece and she hasn't been driven to the point of insanity by the assholes surrounding her.

"Pyro. Come meet these two," Luka calls, pulling me by the arm to the two vamps standing hand in hand. They look extremely similar, too similar to be holding hands. "Alexander and Alexis, meet Pyro, my beloved's third mate. Pyro, meet Alexander and Alexis, the twincest vamps and my closest friends."

Alexis trots over, her gait bouncy and excited, enveloping me in a forced hug. The woman smells of blood and death, a predator wrapped in something sweeter with skin cool as ice. She pulls me in, whispering in my ear. "Keep him safe, you hear? Or else."

Alexander hauls her away, putting his hand out for me to shake. It's firm, dominating until I grip harder, taking over completely. He raises his brow, bowing his head slightly in what looks to be respect.

"You're older than you seem, hound."

My eyes keep flitting over to the VIP, just in case, my focus on Wynn even while entertaining these two. "And you look just as old as I am assuming you both are, fangs."

That moment is when she chooses to make an appearance, my perfect little Wynn, and fuck, does she look breathtaking. Luka grips my arm, shooting pain through to my shoulder. It's bruising and brutish, but it's obviously what he needs. I'm surprised he isn't seeking the connection through his fanged friends, who have stepped into the crowd in front of us.

Everyone looks up at her, marveling at her beauty. Every set of eyes focuses on the perfection that is Wynn. Her dark hair is styled, hanging down one shoulder. The black lace clings to her body, accentuating every single curve. She's confident, despite being in a room full of beings who could tear her to shreds with their bare hands—she's human in a room full of demons and creatures.

Long, claw-like nails grasp the black banister, pulsing at the metal beneath her palms. She is angry at something we can't hear, her stunning features pulling into a scowl at someone behind her. Fuck, she is cute when she's angry.

Her dress is off the shoulder, exposing the mark Bale made across the delicate skin of her collarbone, one now paired with something fresher, the crimson bite is a stark difference against the cool tones of her skin.

"Pyro. She's hurt," Luka all but whines beside me, his grip tightening the longer we stare. "We need.."

I don't let him finish the sentence, because part of me agrees. We need to get her out of their grasp before they have their fill of her and throw us the leftovers. But we can't, not tonight. Not without starting a war and likely getting ourselves killed. As much as I need her, I also need to be alive for her.

"We need to not be dead is what we need. See how many demons are pooled at the bottom of those stairs? All the hellhounds sporadically spread through a club when we are typically not the welcomed species? Lev wanted us here, but on his terms."

Luka looks around, defeat washing over him with each one he spots lurking in the shadows. They have us at every angle, no matter what we do. Exactly as I thought. His hand rakes through his already-messy hair, pulling at the roots.

"Let's get as close as we can, then. I want her to see us, to know we are here." He pulls me closer to the stage, moans and screams growing louder with each step as the cage creaks on its chains. She feels us, she has to. Human or not, we are her mates. She knew that back at Blackstone, and she would know it now.

Wynn scans the crowd, edging the top of her body over the banister. I notice a tight necklace around her throat, one that looks almost like a collar, something dangling from the middle —something I will happily rip from her body the moment we have her back.

That moment is when she locks eyes, those stunning blue orbs flitting between the two of us. It suspends reality, the bodies and sounds blurring into one, the sole focus being her. Raw emotion charges between us, potent enough to get me high if I don't regain some shred of control.

We are screwed.

CHAPTER 19
WYNN

They are here. Pyro and Luka stand in the crowd beneath the decadent VIP lounge, their eyes pinned to mine. I look to the staircase down the back, the thought crossing my mind that maybe, just maybe, I could get down there. It would be a risk, but it may be the only chance I get.

My heart skips, the pace rapid as the organ beats through my chest with bruising force. The intense stare from both of them settles deep within my still-aching core, bringing that need back to life. Not exactly the time or place to get turned on. Although, with what's going on in this place, it's unlikely the beings will be able to feel that emotion from me. There are literally five beings on the stage alone being railed by one another, with multiple couples fucking in booths throughout the lower ground.

Axton walks over to me, placing his hand possessively around my waist, digging his fingers into the soft flesh covered in lace. The dress isn't something I would've picked out for myself, but it does look pretty. I am dressed to perfection, not a hair or nail out of place after a horde of women piled into

Axton's room and assaulted me with brushes and tools. My nails are the sharpest they have ever been, a request from me, with points sharp enough to break skin if needed. Not much protection, but it's something.

He leans down, whispering into my ear, his deep voice sending goosebumps across my skin. The words are quiet, low, intended for my ears only.

"I can feel you, little human. My body is in tune with yours. That pretty cunt of yours aches for them, doesn't it? The lust dripping from you is fucking euphoric, almost worth the beating I would take for stealing you away from the show."

My eyes don't leave theirs, scared that if I look away, they will be gone again, lost in a world I am trapped in. This is the second time I have been close to one of them, so close, it almost hurts. My body physically aches from the bones out, more than it did after the run in the forest.

"Look around you, Axton. There is no way for you to tell those emotions are coming from me. Can I... Is there a way to see them? Even briefly," I ask, my voice a hushed whisper.

"Even if I couldn't tell the difference between your human emotion and those of these other creatures, your scent would give you away. It's sweet, addictive. It's mine." His grip hardens, bruising my side as he nips at my ear. The hint of pain does nothing to dull the throb between my thighs. "You could blindfold me, and I would still be able to track your scent to you, even more so now we are mated."

Axton spins my body in his grip, forcing me to look at him, tipping my chin up until my eyes meet his. They are alight, hungry, the green glistening under the strobe lights. He still hasn't answered my question.

"I asked you a question. Is there a way I can see them?" I breathe, my nails biting into his chest. "Please, Axton. I'm being as polite as humanly possible, biting my tongue at your father's snide comments, resisting the urge to gauge his eyes out with my bare hands."

He smiles down at me, leaning closer until his eyes are level with mine. It's no lie; Lev has been keeping his distance for the most part, as though my mere existence pisses him off. I'm a pawn, no more no less. It takes every single bit of my sanity to not react how I want to every time he opens his mouth.

"Even if I wanted to, it is impossible. Half the demons and hellhounds down on that floor are his. One wrong move will end in bloodshed, and I'm not willing to put you in that position. Being around him is enough, but copping his wrath? Wynn, you have seen nothing."

I look away, averting my eyes to where the guys stand, only to find the space empty. Not a single trace of them. The demons on stage are lowered and let out, and three of the five limp to a door toward the back. Not that I blame them—those hellhound dicks are practically the size of my leg. I'm surprised they can walk at all, to be honest. Lights lower while workers remove the cage altogether, setting up for the next act, whatever that may be.

The staircase for the VIP area is forked at the top, separating two lounges: one we are in, and another that goes from black to dimly hued lights in seconds. There, on the couches, sit Luka and Pyro, flanked by two dark-haired beings on either side of them. All four sets of eyes focus on one thing: me.

"Wynn. Don't," Axton snarls as his jaw clenches tight, flaring at the sides. He knows that thought bouncing around in my mind. The fact that there are only a handful of demons separating me from them is a risk almost worth taking.

A cloaked figure ascends the stairs at that moment, veering to our side. It looks almost as though they are floating, their long, black coat gliding along the floor. They pass the demons without a word, the crowd parting, with their hands drawn, as if touching the being would hurt.

I look over at the guys; Luka looks absolutely murderous beside a collected Pyro, who shakes his head, mouthing 'no' at me. Dark shadows dance with the smoke surrounding Pyro, swirling around each other. It has me concerned Bale isn't here; I assumed he would have healed and been back to getting himself into situations just like this one by now.

The cloaked figure approaches me, extending their hand to me. All their flesh is missing, leaving only pristinely white finger bones with wiry strands holding them together. My hand clasps theirs, shaking it lightly in fear that it will fall to pieces without the muscle and skin holding it together. There's a strangely familiar feeling with this being, an energy that has me calmer than I should be when shaking hands with what looks to be a skeleton in a coat.

"Grimm," his gravelly tone rasps as he dips his head down politely. "It's a pleasure."

"Wynn. But if someone invited you here, I'm assuming you know about the star pony for tonight. Sorry to disappoint, but I'm a little too lame to prance around in circles, so you will have to take it at face value. Do you mean Grimm as in Grimm Reaper?"

Out of my peripheral, I see Luka stand, watching from the banister. We must be loud enough for them to hear as well. Axton's grip tightens further, forcing a wince, his finger tearing a hole through the delicate material of my dress.

Grimm laughs, reaching over to trace my face with one of his fingers, the darkness under the hood giving nothing away. I try to pull away, trapped by the iron behind me and Axton beside me, his cold touch reaching my skin. My body tenses, each inhale of air getting more difficult, as though hands are holding my lungs, stopping them from expanding as deeply as they should. Panic starts to spread through my veins, and I forcibly suck in tiny amounts of air, my heart racing.

Axton rounds on me, stepping between myself and Grimm. He creates a barrier while I suck in a few deep breaths, struggling with the sudden rush of air and toppling a little in my heels. My head spins, the room shifting from one axis to the other, the lights making everything worse.

"Don't fret; I was just getting to know her. I wouldn't have let her die. Next time anyone gets close to the girl, protect her earlier. Her life is too fragile for hesitation." His hand reaches back around, cupping my elbow to stop me from falling. "And you, little show pony—you are nowhere near ready for death with so much life left in you."

With my vision still swirling, I look over to where Luka and Pyro sit, only to find everyone missing except for one. The two other beings and Luka are gone, leaving Pyro staring across the gap. A part of me sinks, knowing I may have stood a chance to run through with four of them, but just one is signing a death warrant for both of us. The dark shadows surrounding him are now still, ashy tendrils suspended in mid-air.

"Wynn, come. Kneel here for a moment, would you?" Lev points to the space on the floor between his seat and Axton's, right beside his legs. His eyes look right past me and focus on Pyro instead. A power play. "Axton, you come back too. The show is about to start."

If he thinks I'm about to kneel, he has another thing coming. It's one thing to have me primped and preened, paraded for the masses. It's a show of power, having something that doesn't belong to him. But forcing me to publicly submit to him, after everything he has done? That may just be pushing my restraint a step too far.

Axton wraps his hand around my wrist, dragging me toward the chairs. My heels dig into the floor, but it's not enough to stop him. He doesn't say a single word, sitting down and pulling me into his lap, my back to his front. His body shakes behind me, the tremors wracking through mine as his grip around my waist tightens.

"I asked her to kneel, son, so make her fucking kneel!" he growls from beside us, his tone impatient. "Or I will."

Before I can register what has happened, my body is torn from Axton's and thrown to the floor in a heap, pain slicing through my hands and knees at the impact. My hair is ripped upward, forcing my top half up off the ground, tears welling in the corner of my eyes at the intense sting.

"This is my only fucking warning, Father," I hear Axton from somewhere behind me, anger lacing every single word. "Let her go. Now."

Lev drags me by the hair to where he wants me, my dress catching on something and exposing my bra completely. I reach up to find his wrists, clawing at the heated skin until he releases his hold. The demon's bloodied hands grasp my chin, forcing me to look at him, his smirk making my stomach drop.

"Your dog just got caught by my hounds trying to get to you. They are ripping him apart as we speak. Hear his pathetic howls? That vamp of yours is probably dead too, bleeding out quicker than his body can repair him in the middle of fucking nowhere. One lone soul left to tell his dear father I won." He grins, his emerald eyes alight, swirling behind his jet-black pupils. Yelps and snarls filter through the air, my gut wrenching with every sound, knowing it could be Pyro. "All we needed was you to lure them out, to make them vulnerable, slaves to their instincts with a need to protect your delicate little life. Watching Satan's world crumble is beautiful, and I have you to thank. My perfect little pawn."

Bile rises in my throat, acid flooding across my tongue. He has killed two of them, the men who stormed into my world and forced their dark souls to play with mine, who saw something in me no one else ever has. My heart fucking aches, each beat heavy. Thick tears stream down my face, likely running tracks of the heavy makeup from my eyes to my chin.

Lev wipes his thumb across my cheek before he brings his finger to his mouth and licks the tears.

"You look prettier when you cry."

Without thinking, I latch onto his hand with my teeth, biting as hard as my jaw allows. The metallic taste of blood floods my tongue, my body thrashing as I'm lifted from the floor by my throat. The grip tightens until little stars start to form behind my heavy lids.

Everything around me swirls, the music in the room replaced with yelling and thumping. My hands reach up, clawing at the grip around my neck until I feel the trickle of blood down my fingers. Another set of hands puts pressure on both of my cheeks, making my teeth release the flesh of Lev's palm before he slaps me, and everything goes black.

CHAPTER 20
WYNN

My mind is hazy as I drift in and out of consciousness, a heavy throb pulsing behind my eyes. A cold, calming hand runs down my cheek, over and over until I'm lulled back into complete darkness. The last image my mind conjures is of the seething rage pouring from Lev's vicious snarl seconds before he slapped me and turned the world black.

"Shhhh, shhhh. Take it easy. You need to rest," a feminine voice whispers close, opening my mouth delicately and pressing what feels like skin to my lips. "That's it, Wynn. Let me help."

My tongue floods with a cool liquid, the elixir slightly sweet. Whatever this mystery woman has given me is helping, I think. Her featherlight touch returns to my cheeks, cooling down my feverish skin. Some awareness returns—the way my hip juts into the hot stone beneath me, pain shooting through the bone. A sheen of sweat covers every inch of my skin.

My body is tired, not having the energy to even be stressed about where I am or who in the world is touching me. Taking comfort in the care they give, I lean into her touch, feeling somewhat safe despite my body feeling like absolute shit. Wherever he threw me, I can count on it not being safe, so taking a moment of reprieve before opening my eyes seems like the best route.

"Any moment now you will start to feel like your muscles are being doused in cool water, feeling returning properly to your skin. Try not to freak out too much. I will keep you safe, little one," the feminine voice coos above me, the sound familiar but hard to place. She traces the bite marks on my collarbone lightly just as the feeling starts to rush over me.

Deep below, my skin tingles, almost like that moment when you are about to peak before an orgasm hits. The cold waves flow from my bones out, reaching my skin and forcing my entire body to tremor as I writhe in the woman's hold. She's patient with me, continuing her calm whispers as the icy feeling removes the aches and pains throughout my body as if they never existed. Even the slight sting between my thighs from Axton's size is gone without a trace.

My eyes blur with unshed tears, blinking into darkness as I attempt to sit up. The space I'm in is damp and dark, the strong stench of death and decay lingering in the air. It burns my inner nostrils, forcing the acid in my stomach to line my throat, spilling onto my tongue. You would think growing up where I did, the scent of death would do nothing, the underlying scent extremely familiar, but this is a whole new level. It's as though bodies upon bodies have been left down here to rot, cooking a little in the heat.

The thrum of my heart intensifies, hyper-aware I have no idea where I am or who is around me. Whoever the woman is feels safe enough, but the room is extremely dark. There could be so many creatures down here, waiting to kill the lamb thrown to slaughter.

"Please, I know you are scared, but try to ease that racing heart of yours. You're safe, but I haven't fed in years, and it may trigger my instincts. Steel those emotions, girl. I saw you do it that first day. You can do it again."

I try to steady my breathing, willing my body to rebuild that wall of emotion, channeling the fear. Acutely aware of every sensation, I focus on the single bead of sweat rolling down the middle of my spine, how it pools along the shred of fabric across my lower hip, dampening the material.

"There we go, Wynn. That's it," she purrs, shifting until her cool body is closer to mine. It's strange to feel a being so cold when everything down here is searingly hot. "Do you know where you are?"

I bite into the side of my cheek, trying to place the voice when the memory hits me: visions of Lev forcing me down a narrow hall surrounded by bars and disgusting whispers from the shadows. The woman with the black hair who asked about my bite—it would make sense as to why she traced it moments ago.

"In the cells below the Keep?" I ask, unsure whether to pray I am right or wrong. At least if they threw me in with her, there is some feeling of safety, despite remembering Lev's taunts, comments about throwing me in here with her and watching her destroy me, how beautiful and tragic it would be. At least if I'm with her, there should be bars in place to keep everything else out.

"Yes, I'm Selene. It's nice to finally meet you properly without that asshole hot on your tail. I wish we had met under more positive circumstances and not by you being thrown in here as a tasty bit of bait."

Her voice is calming in its tone, assertive yet feminine. Though I can't see her, there is still an aura of power flowing from her in waves. It's almost like being around the guys, but not in an intimate or sexual way. It's more an unexplainable feeling of safety despite being around something so dangerous. I remember her sharp claws, fangs so long, they slid over her lower lip, the pulsating black veins that track under hungry eyes. A predator in every sense.

"Sorry to be frank, Selene, but why are you being nice to me? I appreciate you not turning me into chow, but I'm confused. What happened while I was blacked out?" I ask, my voice coming off blunter than intended. Her thumb continues tracing light circles on the back of my hand, clearly not bothered by the harshness in my tone.

"My girl, you have much to learn, secrets that have been kept from the world for far too long. Connections the world has no idea about. It will all come to light in time, but know until they come for you, and they will, you are safe in here. I owe them that."

I start to respond, a million questions on the end of my tongue flowing out as a jumbled mess of words that don't make a lick of sense when strung together.

Thankfully, she stops me. "I know you have questions, Wynn. They will all be answered as soon as you are safely outside these walls. Knowing could get you killed, and with my blood running rife through your veins, you would become a vampire like me. As much of an asset as you would be to my kind, your human life has hardly had the chance to thrive in the darkness with those boys of yours."

We sit in silence for a few minutes, a steady drip in the distance the only audible sound. If there is anyone else down here, they're not moving at all; there's nothing but silence and a drip. I wonder how she knows they are coming for me, especially considering at least two of my guys are likely dead by now if Lev was telling the truth.

Tears well in the inner corners of my eyes, mixing with my eyeliner and making them sting. It feels stupid to be in tears, longing for men you hardly had the chance to know. Two weeks ago, I drove down the winding road to Blackstone Academy, stepping foot into a world that excites the hell out of me. A lump forms in the back of my throat as I choke back the tears that sit on the edge, waiting to flow freely.

"I don't know where you got your information, but half of them are probably dead." I pull my hands away from hers, wiping the tears that have started to run tracks down my cheeks. Once they start, they don't stop; my hands and chest are wet in less than a minute. This emotion thing is much easier when the only person you have to live for is yourself. Caring about others only leads to hurt, something I have saved myself from feeling for most of my life, pain beyond the physical.

"They're not dead, Wynn. Hold yourself together. I know you can. All four of them, they are hurt in their own ways, but they're ultimately fine," a familiar voice orders, one I know without a shadow of a doubt. Her voice is beyond familiar, but one that shouldn't be down here in a cage or down here at all.

"Odette! Odette, is that you?" I stand on wobbly feet, walking toward the voice, only to be halted abruptly by metal bars meeting my outstretched hands. My fingers wrap around them tightly, Selene approaching alongside me.

"Yes, my sweet, it's me. They took me months ago, throwing me down here to torture me for information. The prick got mere scraps, bits and pieces of useless information. But he put two and two together pretty quickly, spreading the word about you and what you are to become."

Odette went missing months ago after working for my family for as long as I remember. She held down the fort while we traveled, keeping business running at home while my parents and I trained recruits in mortuary sciences. She was one of the few who showed me a scrap of kindness. She's a human, so her being here makes no sense.

"I can hear those cogs ticking from here. Those boys should be here soon, but the world is different from what you know, Wynn. I'm sure you have picked up on that. You never wondered why I didn't age, despite watching you grow for eighteen years?"

"Odette..." Selene warns, her tone sharp and harsh, unlike when she spoke to me earlier. "That's enough. Don't overwhelm her."

Suddenly, a door swings open nearby, the light cast into the room revealing it's full of creatures, not empty like I thought. Beings big and small all sit silently and watch the door, their heads hung low. Before my mind has a chance to process what's happening, the door to the cell is unlocked, and a set of razor-sharp teeth latches onto my arm.

Miah's ice-blue eyes cut through the darkness, teeth pulling me from the cell, leaving Selene behind. She and Odette stand there, hand in hand through the bars, tears welling in their eyes as I'm hauled out.

"Wynn, go! I will get Axton to safety. You get out of here and run!" Selene calls, grabbing a set of keys from the ground just outside the cell door. Voices rise through the space, yelling and screaming as she moves from one door to another, letting everyone free. This is about to be mayhem.

We run through the barren halls of the Keep, Miah's teeth tightly digging into my forearm as she drags me along faster. My feet stumble, catching on air at the relentless pace she set. If she just let me go, I could run with her. Likely a little behind, but still, a run.

"Miah, just let me run. Let me go, and I..."

"Please, for once, just do as you are told, Wynn. Let me get you to the door, and then you can do whatever the fuck you want," she mumbles around my arm, pushing us even faster. The sound of carnage creeps behind us at a rapid pace—howls and snarls, screams and breaking timber.

Fuck.

CHAPTER 21
LUKA

The stench of blood wafts out the doors of my home while Alexander and I hold Pyro up, his feet dragging heavily behind us. His body will start to heal itself soon, but this is bad. The twins escorted me out of the club, seconds away from running through the demons to get to her.

Regardless of the consequences. One moment, I was pacing the street, and the next, Grimm walked out with a bloodied, beaten Pyro in his arms, his white hands stained black. He warned us, told us to run, that she has eyes looking out for her, that death wasn't in the cards any time soon for my little mate. Something small to take solace in.

There is every chance each word falling from Grimm's mouth is a lie, a mere ploy to get us out of there. But with the state of Pyro, they could have killed us all if they wanted to. So here we are, covered in tar-like blood with the weight of a tall-ass hellhound slumped around our shoulders as he groans in pain.

My father walks down the hallway to greet us, pure rage pouring out of his soul. I've never seen him like this in all my years. Angry, yes, but not this. He's in his true form, over seven feet of demon vibrating with anger. He approaches Pyro, lifts him from our shoulders, and carries him like he weighs nothing at all.

"Get up to your brother's room. Now! I have Pyro, looks like consciousness is coming back. Go!" he growls, shooing me out the door. I run as fast as possible up the flight of stairs, the echo of another set of footsteps behind me. Panic grips me the moment my father's words sink in, the ability to breathe disappearing. This can't be happening.

I stumble through Bale's door, slamming it into the wall with a loud crash, the handle snapping off. Bale lays motionless under the sheets, hooked up to what looks to be a blood intravenous drip hanging from the four-poster bed. A lump forms in the back of my throat, more painful each moment as I try to hold the tears threatening to escape.

"What the fuck happened?" I roar, charging over to the bed and slapping the side of his cheek over and over. Tears roll down my cheeks freely, and I'm barely able to suck a breath into my lungs. "Bale, wake the fuck up!"

"Luka, stop! He's alive. Just, but he's alive!" Alexis tears me from his side and scowls at me, standing between his limp body and mine. "Take a second and listen. His heart is beating, you idiot. He's gonna belt the shit out of you if he finds out you were slapping him across the face while he was unconscious and unable to knock you out in return."

Bale's fingers twitch, as if reaching for something that isn't there, his dark brows knitting. I push past Alexis, my hand slipping into his, gripping it for dear life. As much as the loss of a mate would slowly kill a demon, the loss of a twin would do the same. A whole part of me would be missing, leaving a void of darkness in my soul that will never be light again. Fear grips me as the realization hits: I may lose both halves to my barely beating heart.

"Get her back, brother. Bring her to me," he croaks out, his voice strained and scratchy. We can't, at least not right now, but I'm not going to be the one to tell him that with the state he's in. "He's hurting her, Luka. Our girl. Burnt."

"His vitals are rising much quicker with the drip. I would give it maybe a few hours, and he will be good as new," the demon beside him explains, scribbling something on the clipboard in her arms. I jump, having not noticed her presence in the room at all. "Sorry, didn't mean to cause a fright, Luka. Your father called for the best care the moment he was dragged in here by a wet mutt."

I look to Bale to ask him about it, but his head is tipped to the side, sleep taking over again. By the looks of the blood and bruises littering every inch of him, he needs the rest. I can feel that familiar fury creeping in, seeping through the shock and hurt lingering deep within me. There's only one demon this could have been, and nothing will fucking stop me from ripping his head from his body, not now, treaty be damned.

Sliding open the drawer at Bale's bedside, I pull out that black bit of lace he usually keeps close, tucking it into his fisted hand. His hand contracts around the lace instantly, white-knuckling the material. He may be out of it, but he still finds comfort in her.

Pyro is showered by the time I reach them downstairs, healing a hell of a lot quicker than Bale. Being a hellhound has its perks, I guess.

"I would have offered to help heal him, but I don't think licking his wounds in my hellhound form would go down so well. I can envision it now: my head mounted above his fireplace with a plaque. *Pyro, I'm happy you're dead.*" Pyro laughs, though his anger overpowers any other emotion trying to crack through. He gets an A plus for effort, I guess.

"Cassius tells us we have an hour until we are to meet another hellhound at the rear side exit of the Keep, where

Wynn will be. We get there, extract the girl, and get out." My father nods, looking at each of us to ensure we understand. Next to him stands a hellhound I have never seen before, one I am assuming is Cassius. "We will need a well-thought-out plan to exact our revenge, but your mate needs to be safe before we even consider it."

My father and I fly ahead, side by side, in complete silence. Satan in his demon form is everything you would imagine him to be: terrifying, with large horns and tattered wings. His size alone is intimidating, standing at least a foot taller than my demon form. This is Wrath, a demon on a warpath, a vision of his title. *Finally.*

We land just on the outskirts of Lev's land, waiting for the others to catch up, hidden amongst the tall, charred trees and open flames. Guilt begins to swirl deep in my gut for the excitement thrumming through my body. This is our chance to get our girl back and fuck shit up on the way to her.

My twin may be a bloodthirsty vampire, but the need for destruction and death runs through my veins just as much as it does his. A by-product of our father's genetics—whether it's a blessing or curse is yet to be decided.

"I'm sorry," my father breathes, his eyes cast low. "I will deal with any repercussions of this tomorrow. We get in there and extract your mate no matter the cost. This is the last time Lev will be able to fuck with our family, I promise you that."

The others arrive just as he speaks his last word, all in their demon forms. Alexander and Alexis are behind the hellhounds, hand in hand, not a hair out of place despite running a distance like that. We gave them the choice to bow out of this fight that isn't theirs, Cassius too, but all of them stand here without a shred of hesitation, poised and ready to fight.

"Left side of the Keep through the side door. In and out. Kill anything that tries to stop you, take no fucking prisoners. We get the girl and take her back home, leaving a pile of mutts in our path," Satan orders, the authority unquestionable. He looks to the two hellhounds, Pyro and Cassius, nodding in their direction. "No offense."

"None taken. Let's fuck shit up and get our girl," Pyro grins, his fangs glistening against the smokey darkness of his coat. He walks to stand beside me, leaning his shoulder into mine with a nudge. "C'mon, demon boy."

Adrenaline pulses through me, amping my body up, readying my body for carnage as we weave through the blackened trees as a pack. My father stands at the forefront, myself and Pyro no more than a step behind, the others spread out, flanking us.

The hellhounds come in waves, hitting our wall before being torn to shreds. I can't help but feed on the raw emotion in the group, all of us embracing the bloodshed. Tearing them down within seconds, limbs flying, leaving a trail of smoking ash. At least we know the route out of here easily—like a modern-day Hansel and Gretel, we leave incinerated bodies in our wake.

One manages to knock me down, the two of us tumbling to the ground in a mess of swipes and punches. I end up on my back, his sharp teeth snap inches from me, heat and spit hitting my face. I can't help but grin at the mutt, sliding my razor-sharp tail straight between his thighs while he plays his little intimidation game.

He spews curses as I twist my tail like a corkscrew, grinding through his internal organs, shoving his smoking body to the ground beside me while his insides become his outsides. The guttural howl ripping from his throat stops the others, each of them turning to watch rather than ploughing ahead to clear a path.

Using the anger bubbling at the surface, I grip his maw, splitting his skull from the bottom with ease before he even realizes what's happening. Serves him right for blindly following Lev.. Yanking my tail from his carcass, I toss the bloody head into the pile of dead mutt, cleaning off my tip on a patch of clean, dry fur.

By the time we get to the Keep, we are covered head to toe in black, chests heaving in near unison. I can't count how many hellhounds are now mounds of smoldering soot in those woods, dying for a prince who treats their kind like absolute shit.

It has taken all of me to not get my hopes up at the thought of finally getting her back, the small voice in the back of my mind whispering that this could all be an elaborate setup, a way to kill us all off in one hit. Bale is protected back home, but he's unable to properly defend himself in his current state. It wouldn't be hard to wipe our bloodline from the realm with us exhausted and him on his death bed.

I wait silently, my heart thudding harshly against my ribcage, my eyes constantly scanning the space, watching for any hint of movement now that we are exposed. It feels off, eerily quiet, considering just how close we are to the home base of pure fucking evil.

The twins walk toward us from the treeline, grins spread across both of their faces, fresh blood coating their teeth. They must have fed on each other, building up the strength for the way back. Little freaks are enjoying themselves in more ways than the rest of us it seems.

Suddenly, the door flies open, and a bloodied Wynn is pushed through the gap, a stark white hellhound nudging her forward. It looks like the one usually trailing Axton, her ice-blue eyes welling with tears, forcing steam to mix with smoke.

In a blur of black and porcelain, Wynn barrels toward me with her arms open, slamming the two of us back a few steps.

My arms snake around her tightly, holding on for dear life. Words catch on the tip of my tongue as I struggle to formulate what I want to say to her. Nothing can describe the feeling of having her back in my arms, the tension in my body melting like ice on a hellstone. Pyro approaches our embrace, hooking his head around me and pulling us into the crook of his neck. The hound's body vibrates, the emotion as overwhelming for him as it is for me.

"Come. Let's get you out of here and back to safety" I whisper into her hair, pressing a kiss to the top of her head. Her little arms squeeze my waist tighter, not wanting to let go. I don't know what she has been through here, but this vulnerability gives me an inkling that we are not going to like it.

"Get her home by foot. The more of you around her, the safer it will be. I need to investigate something. Cassius, stick with me," my father directs without an inch of question. "That's an order."

CHAPTER 22
WYNN

Before my mind can catch up on what the fuck just happened, Luka tears my arms from his body with brutal force, lifting my body to his chest. His grip is firm, pulling me into his soaking wet shirt, blood smearing all over my face and hair. My dress is barely attached to my body right now, the tattered shreds whipping around as soon as we start to move.

"You might want to look away, Wynn. Shit is about to get a little ugly. I can smell them from here." Luka grins, looking down at me as he runs. He looks stunningly unhinged, his platinum hair soaked in black, intense red eyes glowing with emotion. Charred trees and flames blur, messes of orange, black, and gray. I try to shift in his hold a little to see more, but he only grips me tighter to his chest, his fingers digging harshly into my flesh. A few bruises to replace everything healed by Selene isn't a bad thing. I kind of like their markings on my skin.

Relief floods me at the realization that at least two of them are alive, and I doubt Luka would be grinning like a maniac if his twin was dead. My trembling hands grasp his shirt, gripping with every bit of strength I have as the ability to breathe properly starts to ease the strain on my lungs.

Snarls, snaps, and yelps fill the air in all directions, thud after thud hitting the ground. All I can do is hold on for dear life and hope that when we stop, everyone has made it to the end of the gauntlet we seem to be running. Even if I could run at the speed they can, which is physically impossible, I have no weapons other than my puny human fingernails, which will do nothing but lightly slice skin. My existence is already enough of a hazard for the beings that get close, the last few weeks have taught me that.

The further away we get from the Keep, the stronger the feeling pulling me back in. Relief that I'm safe and the urge to go back war in my mind. It's as though a lost part of me remains there, a beacon calling out to the parts left behind. The feeling is heavy, like if I was to stand in one spot, my body would be pulled in both directions until I'm torn to shreds.

Luka drops me to the ground, my hip crashing into the sticks and debris below, a sharp pain shooting through my entire lower back. He stands over my slumped frame, his bloodied tail resting on the back of my thigh.

"Wynn, move back. Way back. Alexander, with Wynn, *now*!" Luka snarls, his eyes brighter than I have ever seen them before. I shuffle until my back hits a tree, and a man crouches beside me, his eyes on the trio but his hand on my shoulder. It's cool against my skin, like Bale and Selene's. It shouldn't bring me comfort, but while watching the scene in front of us, it does.

Five giant hounds creep out from the darkness, foaming at the mouth, their lips pulling up into snarls as they approach. I expect a fight, blood and limbs, more of the yelping we heard the entire way from the Keep, but one of the hounds steps forward, his head bowed ever so slightly.

"Come to meet your fate too?" Pyro asks the one in front,

stalking toward the pack by himself. The cool hand on my shoulder tightens, and my muscles tense. Does Pyro have a fucking death wish? We are outnumbered.

"No, I have come here to give you safe passage. We are not all mindless creatures who bow to those more powerful, you know that. You all should." He peers around Pyro, looking at Luka and the woman beside him before settling on me. "Word on the street is, your mate over there has a soft spot for our kind, Pyro. She is worth protecting more than a piece of shit tyrant who inflicts nothing but pain. So go. Take her and fucking run."

The moment the last word leaves his mouth I'm thrown over Luka's shoulder, my ass in the air and my upper body resting between his wings. He swats my ass before running, the loud crack sending painful tingles across my practically bare skin.

My head spins from being upside down for so long, the dull throb at the top of my spine punching my skull with every step he takes. I try to hold the base of his wings to steady myself, but it does little to stop me from rag dolling over his back at this speed. Trees and smoke blur, orange orbs flashing in my vision every so often from lit flames.

"Almost home. Just a few more seconds, and you can rest. I can feel your emotions swirling, Wynn. Take a few deep breaths, and before we know it, we will be safely home in my father's compound."

We pass through what looks to be a set of heavy iron gates, winged demons on either side. They crash shut the moment we pass, the metal on metal clashing through the silence.

"Oh, fuck!" Luka yells, coming to an abrupt stop, his chest heaving. I writhe in his hold, trying to get him to let me down now, but he's hesitant to let me go, slowly lowering my body to the hard ground with his hands firmly holding my waist to stop me from falling.

Before I even have the chance to turn around, I'm hauled into a wall of muscle, one that rumbles the moment my skin hits his. Bale spins me so we are face to face, his hands gripping my cheeks and tilting my head up to look at him. Unwanted tears threaten to escape seeing him, covered in blood but alive. His thumb catches the first tear to break the seal, licking the remnants while keeping his bright amber eyes on mine. The intensity has me choked, struggling to force out the words.

"I thought you were dead," I whisper, barely audible, watching the black veins spindle around his eyes. He tracks every single tear that rolls down my cheeks, as if it's the most beautiful thing he has ever seen. It's so unlike the Bale who was more than happy to tie me to a tree and feed me to hellhounds weeks ago, the one who told me I would be gone in days. "He said.."

"Even if I was, it would take more than death to keep me from you," he growls, his grip pulsing, as if he's trying to stop himself. He's strained and shaky, unable to contain the need to be closer to me.

"As beautiful as this cute little reunion is, I need our girl for just a moment, brother. Fuck off and leave us be, and then you can take her up there and do all those dirty little things you have been jacking off to for the last few weeks, okay?" Luka laughs as his hand slides around my waist. "You too, pup. Don't think I don't know. Give me five, and I will be out of your hair."

Reluctantly, the two of them take a few steps back, standing side by side, waiting for whatever Luka has to say. He blocks them from my view completely, turning us until his back faces them. A grin spreads across his face as the two of them voice their annoyance, snarls and low rumbles coming from their direction the moment I'm blocked from their view.

"You are safe here, Wynn. Take some time to breathe. Let them dote on you, take care of you. Still give them hell, by all means, but let them care for you in the way they know how." He leans down, pressing his forehead to mine, sucking in a deep breath. "I need to go back, make sure my father isn't dead on a spike. If he is, I will be forced to become him: a leader in a job I want nothing to do with, torn away from you."

I say nothing, not sure how to form the words sitting on the end of my tongue. This need, it's new to me. The small part of me that wants to tell him to stay despite everything else tells me to push him away. He senses my hesitation, his wicked grin widening at my anguish. It's torturous, a man who looks as though he was formed as an angel covered head to toe in blood. Warmth spreads through my stomach at the sight of him, delightfully fucking murderous.

"I want to be able to savor the taste of you, Wynn, to force you into rapture as you cry out my name so the depths of Hell know who you're fucking. You deserve my whole and complete focus while we bond properly, not like the woods."

He leans in and bites my lower lip before I even realize what's happening, his eyes rolling back at my blood flooding his tongue.

"You taste fucking divine. Tomorrow night, Wynn. You and me. None of those fuckers are coming in. Now, go, relish in the treatment you're going to get tonight, because fuck knows if these assholes will do it again."

Their home is huge, luxurious, with large floor-to-ceiling windows in every room we pass, illuminated by the reddened moon. Bale's hand firmly wraps around mine, hauling me through the halls too quickly to truly take in any of it. Doors slam open and kick shut, echoing through the vast space until the three of us end up in what looks to be a bedroom.

It's darker in here, everything in eyesight black. Where the windows we passed are modern, here it's more like Blackstone Academy, with tall arches and intricate details. The four-poster bed sits against one of them, draped in black satin and furs. This is literally heaven. Heaven in Satan's home, but heaven, nonetheless.

Pyro shifts beside me, a swirl of smoke and movement before it thins out, revealing him in all his glory. My eyes drift from the floor up, taking everything in. He's covered in tattoos, the designs rippling over his muscular frame.

My mouth literally salivates at the sight of his cock twitching against his thigh, adorned with metal studs in rows along the bottom of it. The heat already blooming through my core intensifies, thinking of how they would feel gliding against my insides. It's huge, thickening closer to the base.

"You could have given her a second before you appeared naked, asshole," Bale sneers from the other side of me, his hand still wrapped tightly around mine. Pyro smirks, winking at Bale before heading through a door along the wall, the sound of water running starting moments later.

"You can scent her too, right, Fangs? Pretty sure she doesn't mind seeing me naked," he laughs from the adjoining room. Steam flows freely through the door frame, the mist light in the darkness of the room.

My cheeks heat, watching the way Bale's eyes catch on the panties barely covering my pussy. He drinks me in, running his gaze down my body and back up again while his fang toys with the hoop in his lip.

"Keep running your mouth like that, and you can sleep outside. I'm sure the demons won't mind building you a cute little house with your name across the front," Bale snarls back, pulling me toward the door. This dynamic between them intrigues me, the push and pull. Pyro pushes his buttons almost the same as I had back at the academy, but Bale seems to like it, in his own way.

The bathroom is absolutely stunning, fit to be in a hellish space with half-burnt pillar candles surrounding a freestanding antique bath in the center. Bale rolls his eyes before running his cool hands along my skin, peeling the remainder of my dress from my body delicately. Goosebumps follow his hands, spreading across my exposed skin, acutely aware of his touch.

Pyro keeps his eyes on me, his expression changing as soon as my soaked panties hit the floor. Fire-lit eyes catch on every single mark on my skin, every exposed flaw, with an intensity that takes my breath prisoner in my chest.

"You truly are the most perfect being I have ever laid eyes on. Get in the bath before my resolve disappears. I have craved the ghosted taste of you lingering on my tongue for weeks, and I'm famished," Pyro growls, his eyes dancing like lit flames behind obsidian pupils.

Hesitating, I follow his instructions, hooking my legs over the huge tub and sliding my body slowly into the hot water. My eyes roll back at the feeling flooding my skin, the water easing the tension binding my muscles in knots. Blood and soot swirls through the water as I settle in, only just visible, given the only light in here is from the candles on the ground.

"Call us if you need anything. Take some time to breathe. There's some of his nice smelling shit over the other side if you want it. I'm sure he is open to sharing, aren't you, Bale?" Pyro taunts, wagging his brows. He seems more playful when he is more than a step or two away from me, and I want to know why. Before the words leave my lips, the two of them are gone, leaving me completely alone.

Submerging myself fully, I work some of the soap into my hair, letting it sit for a few minutes to hopefully rid the smell of death from it. Smoke and dried blood has seeped into every pore from my time in the cells, and I'm an absolute mess.

Alone for the first time in a while, my mind swirls with

disjointed thoughts, flitting from one thing to the next. Just a few weeks ago, I was Wynn the outcast, thrown into an academy far from home because no one else would have me. I was a girl who thrived in the silence of having no one—it was safer that way. Pain is nothing but a physical reaction of the body, blissfully unaware of how it feels to need another being and the soul-crushing pain of not knowing if you will ever see them again.

Even now, in what feels like a safe place, the anxiety creeps in. Luka is gone again, walking into the bloodied chaos of Lev's home now riddled with prisoners. Beings that have been locked away for god knows how long. He's in danger there, regardless of how strong he is. Then, there's my other mate.

A lump forms in my throat, and I'm unable to swallow the feeling that the club may be the last time I see him. My stomach clenches, a sob wracking through my body before the tears fall. The two I thought were dead are alive, but the other two may very well be six feet under by the morning. How the fuck is one supposed to process that? The loss of someone who owns a deep part of you, who filtered their way through your exterior, only to bury themselves deep within your soul.

CHAPTER 23
WYNN

After a few tears and a long, heavenly soak in the water, my skin and hair are almost free of the last twenty-four hours. Voices sound on the other side of the door, but I can't make anything out. Whatever it is seems heated, though.

Stepping through the door, I see Pyro leaning up against the four-poster bed, his hair wet, a pair of gray sweatpants slung low on his hips. Black and gray tattoos cover almost every inch of visible skin, drawing me in for a closer look. My fingers itch to trace over them, to learn every single line.

Bale halts his pacing as soon as he notices me, his intense scowl softening ever so slightly. Whatever they are arguing about has them both tense and on edge, staring at me as though I have interrupted something serious between them.

"Don't stop your lovers' squabble because I'm here, boys. If someone brings me popcorn, I will even stay and watch." I attempt to hide the emotion welling close to the surface, threatening to take over if I don't hold up that wall with everything left in me.

Pyro senses it, closing the space between us in a few steps, his hand finding my jaw. Bale follows suit, closing in behind me and leaving me sandwiched between the two of them. His nose runs along my shoulder and up my neck, sending shivers across my skin. The coolness of his touch is a stark difference to my flushed, post-bath temperature.

"We are arguing about you. It's driving me mad to not taste you, to not have your life force running through my veins. I want to feed from you, just a touch. Enough to settle the vampire side of me to see straight." He nips at my ear lightly; not hard enough to draw blood, but enough to start that simmering heat that comes with pain. Especially pain that comes from them. "But Fido here thinks you need rest."

"You need some rest, Wynn, some time to process all this shit that has gone down. Trust me, I would love nothing more than to show you how much I need you. But you need some strength in that human body before we go fucking breaking it," Pyro growls, pressing a surprisingly gentle kiss to my forehead.

"What about what I want? What I think?" I ask, trying to slip out of their hold but failing miserably. Their grip on my flesh tightens, giving me no wiggle room at all. The distraction of being bitten and filled to the fucking brink sounds like exactly what I need to calm my mind from the self-deprecating hole it has decided to find comfort in.

"What if I need a distraction? Something to settle my racing mind enough to process what the fuck is going on? What if I need a little of Bale's brutality and to see how much you need me?"

"You're playing with fire here, Wynn. Fire that can get you killed, and we have only just gotten you back. This asshole has exactly zero self-control and made you pass out the first time he fed on you. I have no idea if I will be able to hold myself back enough to not kill you." Pyro steps back, concern written all over his face. As much as I appreciate his concern, the fear of death is the furthest thing from my mind. If I die in the throes of pleasure, at least I die happy. I'm already in Hell; how much further can I truly fall?

"You are saying no in one breath but exciting our little mate the next. You think telling her you might lose control will make her walk away and have a restful night's sleep?" Bale chuckles behind me, a rare noise coming from him. He moves until his head is level with my own, looking at Pyro in front of us. "Tell him exactly what you want, in detail. Give him the explicit consent he seeks."

Standing straighter, I roll my shoulders back before stepping toward Pyro with every inch of confidence my body can muster in this moment. He scowls at Bale, his lip pulling up, revealing his sharp canines. Even in this form, he feels dangerous, like one wrong move could hurt me. A darkness to get lost in, letting my own out to play. Both of them are beings that will consume me whole, relishing in the state of my soul.

"I want Bale to feed on me, with you keeping watch to make sure he doesn't get carried away." His jaw tightens, flaring at the sides. He's not liking what I have to say, but that doesn't stop the need pulsing through me. "Then, I want you to show me exactly how my big, bad hellhound eats before filling me with every single inch of that studded cock I saw earlier. Bale can watch to make sure you don't cover the walls with my flesh."

That does it, flicking the switch I had a feeling was lingering just below the surface, removing the invisible tether of his so-called resolve. The smoke swirls right in front of me, hiding him from view before he tears out of the haze in his hellhound form. He circles me like a hunter does his prey, stalking me, forcing my steps back until my knees hit the edge of the bed, Bale right beside him.

My heart races as Bale places his hands around my waist, throwing me onto the center of the bed. The fluffy towel around my body is torn and discarded on the floor somewhere, Bale hovering over me in seconds.

"One wrong move, Fangs, one single drop more than you need, and I will not fucking hesitate," Pyro growls, snapping in Bale's direction. Bale is completely unphased, focused only on me. Black veins spread from his glowing amber eyes, pools of liquid gold. His fangs descend, sharp and white, terrifying in the best kind of way.

I'm ready to feel that rush again, the feeling of my life both hanging in the balance and being utterly safe all at the same time. He leans down, licking over the mark on my collarbone before sinking his teeth in. Pain and pleasure collide, forcing a moan from my lips as my hips roll to Bale's length, chasing any friction I can get. Tears stream down my temples into my hair, my body so close to coming from his bite alone.

Bale breaks free, moving himself down my naked body until he settles between my legs. His hands grip my thighs, pushing them as wide as they will go before he spits a mouthful of my blood straight onto my exposed pussy. Looking up at me with hooded eyes, he grins manically, crimson dripping from his blood-covered mouth. This has to be one of the most erotic sights I have ever seen in my life, carnal and raw.

He dips down, his tongue swiping through the mess, cleaning the blood with a hum vibrating through him. My fingers run through his messy black hair, gripping it at the root as I grind myself into his mouth. He chuckles against my sensitive heat, sinking his fangs in on either side of my clit before devouring me.

Sharp, black claws dig into the flesh of my thighs, small rivulets of crimson dripping from each indentation as he leans in closer. I teeter on the edge of rapture, my body trembling beneath his firm hold. Just as I hit that peak, he pulls away, smirking at me with blood-stained lips. *Fucking asshole.*

"Your pussy mixed with blood is my new favorite flavor. Now, show her how her big, bad hellhound likes to feast," he orders, sliding off the bed. His eyes pin on Pyro, who is unmoving beside me, plumes of smoke swirling around him.

Pyro circles the bed, crawling between my thighs with his front legs settling under each of mine before he inhales deeply. The power I feel, laying here with him between my thighs, is unexpected. Something so dangerous that it could bite me in half, looking at me like he wants to consume me...

He licks lightly between my thighs, a low growl ripping from his throat before he thrusts his tongue inside my trembling core. Embers spark from his coal-like eyes, glowing brighter the longer he tastes me. His jaw opens wider, his tongue sliding deeper inside me as his sharp teeth rake over my lower stomach and ass.

Holding me between his jaws, he fucks me with his tongue, flicking up to reach that spot inside me that has my hands white-knuckling the sheets beneath me. Intense pleasure burns through my entire body, the feeling like I need to pee sitting right on the edge. Pyro suddenly pulls out, panting through clenched teeth, the fire burning brighter than I have ever seen beneath his coal-like eyes.

"I need to shift before I ram myself so fucking deep inside you, the sheer size splits you in two," he snarls, shaking his head. Before he has a chance to shift, I sit up just enough to see, and my mouth goes dry. Bone fucking dry.

Jutting up between his back legs is a cock almost as wide as my forearm, the base of it sporting a swollen band that looks painfully red. The piercings are still there, barely visible but there. Crawling up until he hovers over my body, he lets his cock rest on my stomach, precum marking the middle of my chest.

"You really think your body can fit this? It's a fucking monster in its own right. If I slam this inside you..." He thrusts it forward for dramatics, the tip brushing my chin. "It will rip through your body and out your mouth. You will die, and I don't have the control in this form to stop that happening."

A blush spreads across my cheeks at the sight. He's massive and likely right. It doesn't stop my body arching off the bed to get closer to him or my pussy clenching at the thought of how full I will be if he does try. My tongue darts out, dragging along the tip, tasting him. The move forces a raspy growl from the hellhound now baring his teeth above me.

His lip pulls up into an angry snarl, but his hips roll forward, edging the tip through my parted lips. The stretch is intense, a barbell hitting my tongue before his tip hits the very back of my throat, my gag reflex kicking into gear. He is so fucking huge, only his tip fits comfortably in my mouth. Holy shit.

My tongue swirls around the tip, hollowing out my cheeks, licking and sucking every inch my body allows. This can't be enough for him, but he hasn't tried to stop me yet. I sneak a peek, looking up through my lashes to find him with his head thrown back.

"You can fuck that uncertainty off, Wynn. You are the first to touch me like this in my hellhound form. Fucking." He rolls his hips again, forcing a little more of himself into my mouth with a groan. "Perfect. You are so fucking perfect."

The praise blooms through my chest, pushing me harder, devouring him. His cock pulses, my hands exploring what I can't fit into my mouth. It practically vibrates in my hold, my fingers unable to meet when I wrap my hand around it. Collecting the mix of precum and spit, my hands glide over his piercings with a firm grip.

Suddenly, he tears himself from my mouth, settling between my thighs, the head of his cock at my entrance. My teeth bite firmly on my lower lip, and I arch up so the tip of him slides in, stretching me immediately. Pyro shakes his head, shifting into his human form before slamming his cock inside me to the hilt.

My breath catches in my throat, the ability to breathe leaving me completely at the intrusion. He unleashes, setting a punishing pace while his hands grip my waist. Each drag of his cock brings me closer to the edge both these assholes have dangled me off, leaving me a whimpering mess.

He pulls out, manhandling me until I'm on all fours, my ass in the air as he slams back inside me. My scalp tingles blissfully as he wraps his fist around my still-damp hair, forcing me to look ahead. Bale is sitting in a wing-back chair, his face covered in my blood. His hand glides down the length of his cock as he watches the two of us with pure need.

The veins throb under his eyes, his sharp fangs piercing his lower lip to hold back the sound. Fresh blood cascades down each side of his chin, dripping onto his hard cock as he chases his release. My mouth waters at the sight of him, powerful and deadly, pleasuring himself to fill a need with his eyes pinned on mine. He moans, his hands gripping tighter, teetering on the edge of oblivion.

Blackened smoke swirls around my throat, tightening as though there is a hand there. Pyro has one hand in my hair and the other on my hip, so it confuses the hell out of me. He chuckles at my squeak, the smoke putting pressure in just the right places while the slower strokes of his cock tease out my pleasure.

"She likes watching you fuck yourself, Fangs. I can feel her pulsing around my cock," Pyro taunts, his smoke biting into the skin of my neck. "Deny it all you want, but the lust pouring from you is almost as potent as hers. Do you enjoy watching our girl getting choked, huh? Hearing her moans every time my cock slides inside her?"

"*Fuck*!" Bale snarls, his release covering his stomach and

chest, his muscles twitching. It starts to drip, glistening under the low lighting. He stands, walking over to the bed with a smirk on his face before grasping my chin and tilting my face up.

"Tongue out," he orders, his voice cracked and raspy. Wanting to see where this goes, I comply, my tongue darting out between my lips. "Good girl. Now, lick. Clean up the mess I made because of you."

He lowers himself a little, allowing me better access with Pyro inching my body forward each time he slides himself back inside me. The salty taste floods my tongue, tracing every ridge of his toned stomach as directed by Pyro's firm grip on my hair. Bale runs a finger through his release, dragging it along his tongue while he looks at something above me. He stares for a moment before returning to his chair, his cock still hard and resting against him.

"Is this what you fucking need, Wynn?" Pyro growls through clenched teeth behind me, struggling to hold himself back. I can feel the hesitation every single time he rolls his hips, but I need it all. I need to feel the raw power flooding through my veins, to be fucked savagely, my body used.

"Stop holding back and use me, Pyro. I want you to fucking use me!" I scream as his grip on my hip tightens and he forces the base of his cock inside me. The sharp pain pushes me over the edge, my pussy tightening around him as my release drips down the insides of my quivering thighs.

"Remember your words when you can't fucking walk tomorrow. Your body fell apart at me just pushing my knot inside you, but I'm about to fuck you with it until I explode. Locking this perfect cunt to me."

That's all the warning I get before he does just as I ask, using me in the most brutal way he can. His enlarged knot pushes past the resistance, stretching my drenched pussy over and over, my body forced forward with each powerful thrust until I'm about to fall from the bed.

Tears flow freely down my cheeks, my body shaking as pleasure rolls through me in waves. I don't know when each orgasm ends or begins, my entire body alight with pleasure and pain, the perfect combination of my two favorite things.

Pyro growls, dropping his hand from my hair to waist, impaling me on his cock with brute force. It pulses painfully, the base much larger than it was before, filling me so much, it burns. My core clenches around him, the intense pain squeezing the last throes of pleasure from my body, mixing my release with his.

Attempting to talk between breaths, I manage broken words, my voice barely a whisper.

"Exactly what I wanted."

I try to collapse onto the soft sheets, Pyro's cock keeping my lower half suspended, his knot locked inside me. He chuckles, laying behind me to hold me close, his arm snaking around my stomach.

"Rest, Wynn. We will take care of you."

CHAPTER 24
BALE

I sit for over an hour, listening to her resting heartbeat, watching the way her chest rises and falls with each breath. My perfect little addiction flows through my veins, her life force combining with mine.

Luka walks into the room with an angry look that softens when he lays eyes on her. Sprawled out across my king-sized bed, cuddled into some of the soft furs, she snores lightly, shifting to face the other way, her ass poking out of the sheets.

"Now that's one way to cheer me up," he laughs, his gaze lifting to Pyro, who emerges from the bathroom. "I'm assuming she got the welcome home she deserves, then?"

"You will have to ask our little mate when she wakes up," Pyro responds, rifling through my drawers like he owns the place to find some clothes. After her reaction to his hellhound getting rowdy, it's no wonder he chooses to walk around in his more human form. He's less of a slave to his primal nature that way, instead of one who wants to sink deep inside our little mate and rut the daylights out of her.

He slips into a pair of my black jeans, the fabric extremely tight over his thighs. "The fuck? I need to get some more shit if she is going to keep making me shift like that."

"Before anyone asks any questions, we need to get downstairs, all of us. Wynn included. Some shit went down and, uhh...well. Things just got a lot more complicated," Luka orders, distracted by her slight movements beneath the sheets.

My fangs toy with the piercings in my lip, thinking about what could have my brother looking this angry and concerned. He's alive; my father's booming voice is faintly audible from here, so I'm assuming he is too. Walking over to Wynn, I pull at the sheet, revealing her pale skin. There's a thin crimson slice running down her spine that looks gnarly, risen and red around the very edges. Pyro might have to beast out a little more with her later.

"I know you are happy to have her back, brother. We all are. But this is time-sensitive and involves us all in some way. If you shoved that knot of yours inside her while siphoning her lust, Pyro, it includes you too," Luka throws at Pyro, who's lacing up a pair of boots beside him.

I bite into my cheek to stop the slew of words currently sitting on the tip of my tongue; none of them would do me any favors. Everything that means a shred of anything to me is inside this room, so whatever this shit is, it's of no importance to me in the slightest. If she's in danger, we get her out of it. If anyone is after her, we slaughter them. No fucking brainer.

Luka crosses the room in long strides, his feet hitting the floor heavy. He reaches to touch her, sliding his calloused hand along the smooth flesh of her thigh. Goosebumps skitter across her bare skin; even in slumber, she's reactive to our touch.

He shifts her so she's lying on her back, her hair blending in with the darkness of the sheets. Moving between her thighs, he flicks his forked tongue out, swiping through the mixed releases with a hum. If my twin notices it's hers and Pyro's mixed together, it doesn't seem to bother him.

Nipping at her clit, he uses his tail to lightly trace the peaks of her nipples, leaving light red lines with each touch. She starts to stir beneath his hold, her hands reaching to rub her sleepy eyes while her hips chase Luka's tongue.

As if only just realizing it isn't a dream, she sits up, swatting his platinum hair hard with an open palm. He only grips her thighs tighter, red marks with white rings blooming on her pale skin from his fingers.

"Lay the fuck back down and let me feast, Wynn. I need to taste you," he growls, face still buried tight between her thighs. Pyro sits in the chair I was in last night, his zipper undone, cock hard against his stomach.

"So much for time sensitive, huh, brother?" I grin, attempting to ignore the hellhound dancing his fingers along his piercings. If he's not careful, I will rip the fucking appendage off. In the last few weeks, I have seen his dick more than my own.

"What, Fangs? Like what you see? Your jeans are too tight to be sporting a hard-on. This..." He gestures to a now-whining Wynn writhing under my brother's touch. "No way I could keep it down with this in front of me. Sorry."

The only response I get from Luka is his middle finger aimed at me, not moving a muscle from his task at hand. By the whimpers coming from the bed, it's a task he is doing decently at least.

Shaking my head at him, I look back just in time to see her explode, back arched off the bed, sharp nails drawing blood from Luka's scalp with a scream. Her chest heaves, a glistening sheen of sweat covering her now-blushing skin.

"I will never tire of the taste of you. Ever. You are so fucking perfect," he whispers, planting light kisses from her pussy to her throat.

"Now, pretty girl, there are some demons downstairs waiting to see us. You are going to need to throw some clothes on," he explains as he climbs off the bed to riffle through my drawers too.

Throwing a black t-shirt and a pair of black boxer shorts on the bed, he stares at me intently, his brows furrowed.

"And you."

We walk down to the lounge as a group with Luka at the front, the three of us walk behind him. Interlacing my hand with hers, I almost expect her to shoo me away or spit some sort of venom my way with her words. But she grips me tightly, becoming tense the closer we get. Voices filter through the walls, masculine and feminine, not all of them familiar.

What I find in the space has me stopping in my tracks, physically unable to move. Pure rage floods my veins, and I drop her hand before my claws slice into her, digging them into my own palms instead. She stays beside me, her eyes flitting between the two beings on the other side of the room and me.

Pyro moves to stand to my other side, his arm resting against mine. It should piss me off more than it does, but in this room, he is the lesser of evils. Not that I would ever admit it to him, but it brings me comfort knowing I have not only my twin and Wynn by my side, but this furry asshole as well.

Looking at the woman standing opposite me is like looking into a mirror, one reflecting a gaunt female version of myself. Her eyes are slightly sunken, the veins around the amber orbs black and painful looking. She goes to open her mouth, suspending whatever it is she wants to say.

Axton stands beside her, covered head to toe in blood and soot, scowling at the three of us until his eyes settle on her—

emerald eyes I will happily pluck from his fucking skull once my body decides it can move freely again.

"Someone care to explain to me what the fuck is happening?" I snarl, looking between the newcomers and my father, who is standing off to the side, still in his demon form. He's a mass of muscle and tattered wings, looking utterly defeated.

Surprising everyone, me included, Axton is the one to step forward and start talking. The words coming out of his mouth spark a raging inferno that will take every single shred of my self-control to tamper down.

"This woman is your mother." He points to the woman beside him, his eyes still pinned on my mate. "Here's the kicker, though, vamp boy. She's also mine, just like the little human you have there. Mine."

Wynn grips my arm, willing my more primal side to seek her out rather than create the carnage it desires. It's not the first time I heard him refer to my girl as his own, but there was hope he just said shit to piss me off. If he isn't lying, we're about to have one hell of a fight on our hands, one that can no longer lead to the slow and painful death I was planning for him. Fuck.

Tears start to fall down the woman's cheeks as she struggles to keep her composure. I look over at my twin; he looks just as murderous as I feel. His jaw is set, red eyes staring straight through her. He has had more time to process all of this, but that doesn't mean he's not as pissed.

"Explain," I snarl, sounding more animal than man. The word barely makes it past my clenched fangs. None of this makes any sense; my mother ran as soon as she gave birth. This waif of a vampire can't be the royal bloodline my father speaks of. She looks moments away from death, as if the soul has been sucked out of her for years on end.

My father takes a step toward her, opening his mouth to

speak, but she cuts him off, building the courage to come closer to us. She takes her time, looking both Luka and me up and down, settling on Wynn at my side.

"You look beautiful, Wynn, so full of life." The woman reaches out to Wynn, but she stops the second she hears a snarl from all three of us.

"Selene, I am so fucking glad you made it. You should have told me who you were. It would have made so much more sense." Our girl smiles in response, hugging my arm. Her heartbeat remains steady; she doesn't see the woman as a threat. Interesting.

Selene reaches her hand out, placing it across my beating heart, and my entire body shakes to control itself. If this is, in fact, my mother, why am I not ripping her cold, dead heart out for leaving me in the hands of my father?

Luka makes his presence known then, grabbing her arm and pulling it from my chest, shaking his head. "Don't push too hard too fast. With him or me. My brother is seconds from ripping your heart from its cavity, leaving all three of us just as motherless as we were yesterday, Selene."

She sighs. "I tried to come for both of you. I tried so fucking hard to escape. After Axton was born, I almost made it out of the Keep, him in my arms. But Lev had me hunted down and dragged back to the cells. He killed all the hounds who knew I was there, all bar one." Her rolling tears turn to sobs, racking her entire body with shuddering breaths. "I spent years wasting away in the bottom of the cell, taunted, teased with sustenance only for it to be left just out of reach. After years, I lost hope. I was destined to die in darkness. Alone."

My father takes this moment to approach her, his hand tentatively falling to her lower back. For the first time in my entire life, I feel my emotions replicated in the demon who sired me: complete and utter fucking conflict.

"That is, until a sweet little demon was tossed down there with me, speaking fondly about a girl with onyx hair and an attitude like no other. She had visions of the girl with several powerful mates." She shifts her gaze to Wynn, who stands with a grin across her face. "A human to protect at all costs."

My mind is at war, rage and hurt clashing together as I grip Wynn's hand like my life depends on it. She squeaks beside me but doesn't pull away, leaning into my grip. The rest of the room is silent, no one else says a goddamn thing until him.

"If you hurt her, Bale, even a little, I won't hesitate to tear you to fucking pieces," Axton seethes, stepping closer. Ballsy to threaten me in my own home, flanked by two demons who wouldn't hesitate to jump in should the need arise.

I lean toward him, a grin spreading across my face, showcasing my fangs. "You wouldn't dare. If you kill me, it hurts her, causing a world of internal pain she may not even live through. I would love nothing more than to rid Hell of your existence, but here we are."

Pyro is the one to interject, stepping between the two of us, one of his hands on my upper arm. He looks between us, his jaw tight. Part of me wants to throw his hand off me, the heat painful. The other part, though, feeds off the connection.

"I'm hardly even involved in any of this shit. Everyone needs to calm down a little and think of the threat. There will be plenty of time for family bonding after we sort everything out. This is about to rain down on Hell in epic proportions, changing everything. The treaty is fucked, many are dead, and we are harboring the son of the enemy," Pyro snarls, his grip tightening.

"My father ran, and until he is gone for good, none of us are safe now that everyone will know his secrets. He will stop at nothing," Axton warns, his focus solely on Wynn. "We are going to need to sort some shit between us, or we risk him killing off the one thing that will destroy us all."

"Then we destroy him first," Wynn chimes in beside me, her eyes searching mine. She doesn't even realize the carnage we are willing to rain on the underworld to keep her safe, but she's about to.

The End....for now.

ACKNOWLEDGMENTS

First off, I would like to thank YOU. Thats right. You.

For not only reading my debut, but coming back for another round. I truely have the most amazing readers, and wouldn't be here for the second time if it wasn't for the support I received after my first release. I value each and every single one of you.

My ride or dies. The ones who have dealt with the tears, the hundreds of voice notes riddled with self-doubt. This book wouldn't be here without you either. Angelica, Kristy, AK, Lauren, Mel and Rach, you have all played such a huge part in me getting this book to the finish line and I am forever thankful! From reading snippets, to diving into my doc head first to leave me love notes. Every single bit helped.

My editor, Elisabeth. A saint of epic proportions. Who saw my vision and encouraged it to run wild. I absolutely adore you, and the work you have put in to make my baby shine.

And my Alpha and Beta readers. The ones who saw my ugly and loved it anyway. Amanda, Katelin, Phylicia, Charmaine and Zoe. Your input was worth its weight in gold and Chained wouldn't be what it is today without you. Thank you for all of your feedback, and for giving me the boost I needed to keep going.

About the Author

K.L. Steele is a dark paranormal romance author from Victoria, Australia. She loves reading dark, trusted love stories and collecting book boyfriends who are a step beyond the morally grey.

She is a bit of a genre hopper when she reads, swapping between monster, bully, paranormal and dark romance.

Also by K.L. Steele

Blackstone Gates Series
Locked

Standalones
Bound by Darkness
Festive Fates

Printed in Dunstable, United Kingdom